Ally had counted on the cowboy coming to her rescue.

What she hadn't counted on was being imprisoned between a pair of muscular, jean-clad legs. She looked up to see the cowboy staring down at her with the most charming smile. He was casually straddling the bar stool, one hand resting on his knee, the other still grasping her upper arm with a strength that caught her by surprise.

"Sorry, Red." His voice was low. "Didn't mean to startle you. But I wasn't sure you'd like to find yourself wearing all those drinks."

"Thanks." She reached out a hand to steady herself and came in contact with a chest of solid muscle. Something else she hadn't planned. Even after she moved her hand away and lowered it to her side, she could feel her fingers tingling from the touch of him. Aware of the intimacy, not to mention the awkwardness, of their positions, she took a step back and looked up.

He hadn't been expecting those eyes. Green, with little flecks of gold. Or the reaction he'd felt from that simple touch. Like icy needles down his spine, and then a sudden surge of heat through his veins…

Dear Reader,

Once again, Silhouette Intimate Moments has rounded up six top-notch romances for your reading pleasure, starting with the finale of Ruth Langan's fabulous new trilogy. *The Wildes of Wyoming—Ace* takes the last of the Wilde men and matches him with a pool-playing spitfire who turns out to be just the right woman to fill his bed—and his heart.

Linda Turner, a perennial reader favorite, continues THOSE MARRYING McBRIDES! with *The Best Man,* the story of sister Merry McBride's discovery that love is not always found where you expect it. Award-winning Ruth Wind's *Beautiful Stranger* features a heroine who was once an ugly duckling but is now the swan who wins the heart of a rugged "prince." Readers have been enjoying Sally Tyler Hayes' suspenseful tales of the men and women of DIVISION ONE, and *Her Secret Guardian* will not disappoint in its complex plot and emotional power. Christine Michels takes readers *Undercover with the Enemy,* and Vickie Taylor presents *The Lawman's Last Stand,* to round out this month's wonderful reading choices.

And don't miss a single Intimate Moments novel for the next three months, when the line takes center stage as part of the Silhouette 20th Anniversary celebration. Sharon Sala leads off A YEAR OF LOVING DANGEROUSLY, a new in-line continuity, in July; August brings the long-awaited reappearance of Linda Howard—and hero Chance Mackenzie—in *A Game of Chance;* and in September we reprise 36 HOURS, our successful freestanding continuity, in the Intimate Moments line. And that's only a small taste of what lies ahead, so be here this month and every month, when Silhouette Intimate Moments proves that love and excitement go best when they're hand in hand.

Leslie J. Wainger
Executive Senior Editor

Please address questions and book requests to:
Silhouette Reader Service
U.S.: 3010 Walden Ave., P.O. Box 1325, Buffalo, NY 14269
Canadian: P.O. Box 609, Fort Erie, Ont. L2A 5X3

the WILDES of
WYOMING —
Ace
RUTH LANGAN

Silhouette®
INTIMATE™ MOMENTS®

Published by Silhouette Books
America's Publisher of Contemporary Romance

For my own wild bunch.
Mike (the baby) this one's for you. With love.

And, of course, for Tom. Who gambled and won.

SILHOUETTE BOOKS

ISBN 0-373-27079-8

THE WILDES OF WYOMING—ACE

Copyright © 2000 by Ruth Ryan Langan

This edition published by arrangement with Harlequin Books S.A.

Visit Silhouette at www.eHarlequin.com

Printed in U.S.A.

RUTH LANGAN

Award-winning and bestselling author Ruth Langan creates characters that *Affaire de Coeur* magazine has called "so incredibly human the reader will expect them to come over for tea." Four of Ruth's books have been finalists for the Romance Writers of America's RITA Award. Over the years, she has given dozens of print, radio and TV interviews, including *Good Morning America* and *CNN News,* and has been quoted in such diverse publications as *The Wall Street Journal, Cosmopolitan* and *The Detroit Free Press.* Married to her childhood sweetheart, she has raised five children and lives in Michigan, the state where she was born and raised.

IT'S OUR 20th ANNIVERSARY!
We'll be celebrating all year,
Continuing with these fabulous titles,
On sale in June 2000.

Romance

#1450 Cinderella's Midnight Kiss
Dixie Browning

#1451 Promoted—To Wife!
Raye Morgan

AN OLDER MAN
#1452 Professor and the Nanny
Phyllis Halldorson

The Circle K Sisters
#1453 Never Let You Go
Judy Christenberry

The WEDDING AUCTION
#1454 Contractually His
Myrna Mackenzie

#1455 Just the Husband She Chose
Karen Rose Smith

Desire

MAN OF THE MONTH
#1297 Tough To Tame
Jackie Merritt

#1298 The Rancher and the Nanny
Caroline Cross

MATCHED IN MONTANA
#1299 The Cowboy Meets His Match
Meagan McKinney

#1300 Cheyenne Dad
Sheri WhiteFeather

the Baby Bank
#1301 The Baby Gift
Susan Crosby

#1302 The Determined Groom
Kate Little

Intimate Moments

#1009 The Wildes of Wyoming—Ace
Ruth Langan

#1010 The Best Man
Linda Turner

#1011 Beautiful Stranger
Ruth Wind

#1012 Her Secret Guardian
Sally Tyler Hayes

#1013 Undercover with the Enemy
Christine Michels

#1014 The Lawman's Last Stand
Vickie Taylor

Special Edition

#1327 The Baby Quilt
Christine Flynn

#1328 Irish Rebel
Nora Roberts

Baby Set
#1329 To a MacAllister Born
Joan Elliott Pickart

A Family Bond
#1330 A Man Apart
Ginna Gray

DESERT ROGUES
#1331 The Sheik's Secret Bride
Susan Mallery

#1332 The Price of Honor
Janis Reams Hudson

Prologue

The month of July had been a scorcher. Folks around Prosperous, Wyoming, were saying they couldn't recall a spell of hotter, drier weather. It parched the land, withered the crops, and sent tempers flaring.

At the Double W, it was cause for extra concern. Without the range grass to sustain their cattle, the Wilde brothers had been forced to dip into their cash reserve to buy grain.

It was nearly three in the morning. In his room, Chance Wilde, at twenty-two, the oldest of the three brothers, tossed and turned and tried to escape his worries in sleep.

Twenty-year-old Hazard was hunched over the kitchen table, trying to figure out what he could sell off in order to keep the ranch going. Beside him lay the letter from the county, warning that unless the back taxes were paid within the month, their land would be confiscated.

He and his brothers had been up since before dawn the day before, handling the hundreds of chores around their ranch. The cattle were only a small part of it. There was the well that was threatening to go dry. The ten-year-old truck that demanded constant repairs in order to keep running. The barn roof that had been patched so many times, it resembled, from a distance, a quilt. And the small plane he and his brothers had bought, in order to keep track of their hundred fifty thousand acres of wilderness, that was now crash-landed in a field. They still had two more years to make payments on a pile of twisted metal.

As the figures started to blur Hazard closed his eyes and rested his forehead on his folded hands. As if he didn't have enough to worry about, his younger brother, seventeen-year-old Ace, who had walked away from the crash-landing with nothing more than some scratches, had taken off as soon as his chores were finished and headed into town.

There wasn't much nightlife to brag about in the little town of Prosperous. There was the E.Z. Diner, where the chili was as hot as the weather. For those who wanted to impress a girl from among the church-going families, there was Alice's Ice Cream Parlor. Next door was a small movie theater running films that were already showing on cable. The majority of cowboys headed to Clancy's, to drink beer and shoot pool.

It was on nights like this that Hazard found himself wishing desperately for his father's advice. There was no telling how much trouble Ace would get himself into. Hazard's only consolation was the fact that Clancy had already banned Ace from his saloon until he was old enough to drink. In his freshman year Ace had been tossed out for hustling cowboys at the pool tables and relieving them of their paychecks.

Without the lure of Clancy's there wouldn't seem to be much room for trouble. Except, in Ace's case, trouble always seemed to find him.

Hazard was vaguely aware of the sound of gravel churning as the old truck engine coughed and circled the house before coming to an abrupt halt at the back door. Relieved that the source of his worries was finally home, he started to drift back to sleep when he heard the sound of the horn honking. A continuous, annoying sound that had his head coming up sharply, at the same time that Chance stomped into the room, barefoot and shirtless, snapping his jeans as he did.

''What's that?'' Chance demanded.

''Don't know. Ace, I guess.'' Still half-asleep, Hazard shoved away from the table and followed his brother across the room.

Outside the horn was still blasting, as though someone was leaning on it.

''Shut up.'' Chance was out the door and sprinting toward the truck, hoping to slap some sense into his little brother. He snatched open the door, then froze.

Hazard bumped into him, then stepped to one side to see what had stopped Chance in his tracks.

''What the…?'' It was the sight of Ace slumped over the wheel that brought him up short. That, and all that blood.

For a moment he felt his heart stop. Then he saw the slight movement that told him Ace wasn't dead. Yet. He reached up and dragged him from the truck, ready to throttle him within an inch of his life. ''Give me a hand.''

Hazard caught him under one arm, while Chance

took the other. They managed to haul their younger brother up the steps and into the kitchen, where they lay him on the floor.

"Get some blankets," Hazard shouted as he knelt beside the still form.

His preliminary training in veterinary medicine hadn't prepared him for this. There was blood everywhere. Streaming from Ace's arm, soaking his shirt and jeans. More blood poured from a gash in his head. His face was a mess. His eyes blackened. His mouth swollen to twice its normal size.

Hazard grabbed some kitchen towels and a pan of hot water and began to mop at the blood. When Chance returned with some blankets, he was already at work with a first-aid kit, disinfecting the wounds.

Chance knelt beside him. "Think that wound will close without stitches?"

"I hope so." Hazard drew the two sides of the gaping cut together and firmly applied a bandage. "He's going to have a lovely scar, but his hair will hide it."

"Look at this." As Chance tore away the sleeve of Ace's shirt, his eyes narrowed. He pointed to the gash that was several inches long and gushing blood. "Looks like a knife wound."

"Yeah." Hazard poured a liberal amount of disinfectant, hoping the blade had been clean.

At Ace's hiss of pain he added a few more drops for good measure. "So. You're alive."

"Am I?" Ace opened his eyes and squinted against the glare of the kitchen light.

"Looks that way." Hazard began dressing the wound. "Who did this?"

"The cowboys…" Ace found it hard to speak

around his swollen, bloody lips. "...From the Circle T."

"Why?" Chance's heart was starting to beat again, now that he realized his little brother was going to live.

"They..." Ace wiped a mouthful of blood on his torn sleeve. "...Wanted their money."

"Their money?" Chance's eyes narrowed. "Have you been at Clancy's?"

"You know I'm barred." Seeing that Hazard was finished with him, Ace sat up weakly. For a moment his head swam, before his vision gradually cleared.

"Then where'd you get their money?"

Ace caught the edge of the table and pulled himself to his feet where he stood very still for a moment until he got his bearings. He knew, from the pain, that there were a couple of broken ribs. "Started a crap game behind the bar."

"A crap game." Chance caught him by the front of his shirt. "What the hell's wrong with you? Isn't there enough excitement in your life? Did you think it might be fun to see just how far you could push these guys before they'd push back?"

"Hey." He shoved his brother backward. It was all he could manage at the moment. "I'm still standing."

"Barely." It was Hazard's turn to grab him by the shirtfront. What he really wanted was to knock some sense into him, and maybe bloody his nose again. But he'd just taken all that time and effort, not to mention the toll on his nerves, to patch his brother up. It wouldn't do to have any more bloodshed. "And only because we were here to pick up the pieces. How the hell did you even drive yourself home?"

"Sheer willpower," Ace said with a grin.

"Bullheaded, you mean." Hazard gave him a shove

backward and watched with satisfaction as Ace had to steady himself against the table. "You're just too stupid to realize that those cowboys could have killed you. And all because you had to feed your need to gamble."

"Yeah." Ace was beginning to fade. He could feel it. But there was no way he'd show any weakness in front of his two brothers. Not when they still thought of him as the kid. The youngest. The baby.

It rankled. Always had. Almost from the moment of his birth he'd been fighting for his place in this family. Here he was, a senior in high school, the tough guy on campus, and he still had to take orders from these two.

Chance was fighting a battle against anger and relief. Anger that his precious sleep had been shattered by Ace's foolishness, and relief that his wounds hadn't been more serious. For a moment there…

He fisted his hands on his hips, determined not to let himself think about what might have happened. "The next time you want to go to town, big shot, you can walk."

Ace's eyes widened. "What?"

"You heard me. I'm through worrying about what kind of mess you'll get yourself into. From now on, the truck's off-limits."

"Fine." Ace knew he didn't have much time left. There was a buzzing in his ears, and the faces of his brothers kept swimming in and out of his line of vision. His body felt like one giant toothache.

He reached into his pocket and pulled out a fistful of bills. With as much dignity as he could muster he set them on the table, before staggering like a drunk.

"What's that?" Hazard eyed the money.

"The last I counted, it was fourteen thousand dollars."

"Fourteen…" Hazard turned to Chance, then back to Ace, too stunned to finish his sentence.

Ace managed what he hoped was a negligent shrug of his shoulders. "I really wanted to stay home tonight and finish my geometry." He even managed that famous grin, though it cost him. "But I figured this was more important. I was the one who ruined the plane. And I didn't want you to lose any more sleep over those back taxes. I figure this ought to keep us going for a little while longer."

He walked stiffly away, until he hit the hallway. Then, bent almost double, he limped off to his bed. Leaving his brothers staring at each other in absolute astonishment.

It would seem that their foolish, hotheaded little brother had just saved their hides. As usual, without regard to his own.

Chapter 1

"Cass." Restless, Ace Wilde moved around the cabin of the private jet, holding the cell phone to his ear as he spoke to his assistant. His briefcase, tossed carelessly in a seat, was bulging with documents. He wore his success as casually as his custom-tailored suit, which he couldn't wait to exchange for jeans and a plaid shirt as soon as he got home. "I'm running later than I'd planned. I'm not going to get back to the office in time to look over those contracts. Why don't you fax them to me. And you may as well give me my phone messages. I can return some of them. The rest will have to wait until tomorrow."

His longtime assistant, Cassidy Kellerman, reeled off a list of names and numbers, while Ace scribbled in a notepad. "Remember. You have a nine o'clock appointment tomorrow with a Phillip Curtis from the government."

"Right. Curtis. Thanks, Cass. Send me that fax now."

"Wait. I think you've forgotten something."

When he didn't respond she gave a sigh of resignation. "It's the little matter of my replacement."

"Oh. That. How's she working out?"

"Fantastic. She's smart. Efficient. Fun. But I can't keep her dangling forever, Ace. She needs to know whether or not she has the job."

"Look. I don't have time for this." He huffed out an impatient breath. "As long as you're satisfied with her qualifications, that's all that matters."

"Ace, I'm flattered to know that you trust me on this." He could hear the smile in her voice. Because she and Ace had gone through school together, and had worked side by side for a decade, she was comfortable saying exactly what was on her mind. "But you're the one who'll be working with her. You need time to observe her job skills, and decide whether or not the two of you are compatible. It was your decision not to hire Marla Craine."

Ace frowned, thinking about the girl who had worked in the outer office of WildeMining for the past three years. She and Cass were best friends. But when Cass had recommended her as a replacement, he'd had to refuse. He knew it had come as a shock to Marla as well as Cass. But her job skills weren't even close to those of his longtime assistant.

"Ace." Cass's voice came over the phone line. "The final decision has to be yours."

"Then I'm making it. Hire her."

"Sight unseen?"

"Sight unseen. If you approve, that's good enough for me."

"Okay. But be warned. I don't want to hear any complaints about this later. With all the last-minute things I have to plan for my wedding, I don't have time to go through this again." Her voice warmed. "Just think. After I walk down the aisle with Larry, I'm never going to worry about what goes on at WildeMining again."

"Yeah?" He barely paused before saying, "I still say you're making a big mistake, Cass. I figure it'll take about two weeks after your marriage before you're crying in your morning coffee because you let Larry talk you into quitting. You know you love it."

"Ace, we'll be living two hundred miles away."

"So do I. That's a pretty lame excuse, Cass."

She heard the teasing laughter in his voice and gave it right back. "Yeah. Well here's an even better one. As soon as the honeymoon is over, I expect to be taking my first home-pregnancy test."

His mouth dropped open. "Are you crazy?"

"No. I'm over thirty. And, in case you've forgotten, so are you. That clock's ticking. I want a baby, Ace. And I want one soon."

"Give my best to Larry," he said dryly. "He's going to need it. And Cass, send me that fax now."

He disconnected, then walked to the window to stare at the land below. The plane was just passing over the tips of the Bighorn Mountains. The sight of them glistening in late summer sunlight never failed to give him a thrill.

He and his brothers had worked so hard to make their father's dream come true. But the reality was so much better than anything Wes Wilde had ever envisioned. WildeOil, headed by Chance, the oldest brother, was showing its highest profit ever. The ranch, the Double W, which middle brother Hazard operated, was the largest and most successful in Wyoming. And WildeMining, which was Ace's baby, with its treasure trove of coal and uranium, was quickly becoming a force to be reckoned with.

Still, in some small part of his mind he realized that he missed those lean years. Lately, with all their success, there had been so much change. Their own jet and helicopter, and crews to maintain them. So many additions to the sprawling ranch house that it now looked more like a mansion than a ranch. And additions to the family, as well. Both Chance and Hazard had fallen in love and had recently married.

Marriage. It seemed as though the whole world was on a marriage binge. It wasn't just his brothers. There were his college pals, who were now starting families of their own. And even Cass, his long-time secretary, who was giving up a satisfying career to settle down with a rancher. He shook his head. They'd all lost their senses and were falling like dominoes. Who would fall next?

"Not my problem," he muttered aloud as the fax line hummed.

He tore off the first page and settled himself in the leather recliner, fastening his seat belt as he did. He'd be home in less than an hour. And in town, relaxing over a beer and a game of pool at Clancy's, in less than two.

"Hey, Ace."

"Hi, Boone." Ace slid onto the bar stool beside his

old high school buddy. On his other side sat Cody Bridger, a weathered old cowboy who had been at the Double W since Ace was a boy. The two had driven into town together.

"I never see you in here, Boone. What's the occasion?"

"Barb and the kids went up to Laramie to visit her folks. I've got the weekend to myself."

"A weekend of freedom, you mean." Ace signaled the bartender, who set long necks in front of him and Cody.

"Naw. Truth is…" Boone grinned and took a pull from his bottle. "…I'd rather be home in front of the TV. But the house feels too empty. So I figured I'd kill some time here at Clancy's. See if any of the old gang was here." He turned to Ace, who was already scoping out the pool tables, looking for a game. "You're the only one I know in here."

"That's because I'm the only one who hasn't let himself get roped and hog-tied by a female." Ace shot him the famous Wilde smile before turning again to peer through the haze of smoke.

That's when he spotted the redhead. Despite the pall that hung in the air, she stood out like a beacon with that cloud of fiery tangles spilling down her back. That wasn't all she had going for her. Long legs were poured into tight jeans. A little bit of a shirt had pulled away from her waist to expose just a trace of creamy white skin. Her body, bent over the pool table as she concentrated on the cluster of balls at the opposite end, was almost sinful.

Ace found himself mesmerized by the sight of her

backside. It took him a moment to realize that she'd completely missed her shot. She was laughing about it as she turned away and watched the cowboy beside her take aim.

The cowboy wasn't much better. He tried to show off by banking a shot. The ball bounced off the side of the table and rolled harmlessly to the other end.

The redhead looked up at him adoringly. Then she bent over the table again. Just as she was about to take her shot the stick slipped from her hand, hitting the ball. It rolled across the table and fell into the pocket.

"You get to take another shot," the cowboy said.

"I do? Oh, this is fun." Her voice was unexpectedly low and sultry. Not at all what Ace had been expecting.

"Hey, Benny." Ace was nearly salivating. "Who's the new girl?"

The bartender looked up. "Don't know her. She's never been in here before."

"You sure?"

Benny grinned. "Believe me, Ace. I'd remember that one."

"Yeah." Ace sipped his beer and continued to watch as the cowboy strutted around the table, making a few miserable shots, and accepting praise from the girl who didn't even know which end of the stick to use when it was her turn. By accident she managed to sink another ball, winning the game.

As he handed her some money, the cowboy put an arm around her shoulder and whispered something that had her smiling and looking up into his eyes while shaking her head in refusal.

Ace couldn't help grinning. He turned to Cody, who was watching without expression. "I'll give her this

much. Even when she refuses a guy's offer, she does
it so sweetly he goes away feeling like he might have
another chance.''

Cody grinned and nodded.

Ace watched as the cowboy took a seat across the
room, while one of his buddies stepped up and offered
to teach the redhead how to play the game for twenty
bucks.

Ace turned to his old friend. ''Can I buy you a beer,
Boone?''

Boone shook his head. ''Thanks anyway, Ace. Think
I'll go home and call Barb.''

As he strolled out, Ace turned to Cody. ''Ready for
another?''

''Not yet. Think I'll nurse this one awhile.''

Ace ordered himself another beer and leaned his
back against the bar, watching the second cowboy
make his moves on the redhead. It was proving to be
the best show of the night.

Ally Brady ducked into the ladies' room. After closing and locking the stall door, she pulled the wad of
bills from her pocket and began to count them.

Eighty dollars. Not bad for a start. She'd likely use
every bit of it to make what she needed before she went
home tonight. And she'd located her mark. The cowboy sitting at the bar.

The minute he'd walked in, she'd spotted him. Even
though he was dressed like all the others, in faded den-
ims and a plaid shirt, he smelled like money. His boots
may be dusty, but they were custom. She figured they
cost him a thousand dollars or more. That made him
fair game. She wouldn't be relieving him of his pay-

check. She'd simply be denying him his next pair of luxury boots. That ought to soothe any guilt she might have for what she was about to do.

She grinned and carefully divided the money, putting half in one pocket, the other half in her boot. Then she fluffed her hair, wet her lips, and sauntered back to the pool room.

The crowd had gotten louder. There was a crush of people milling about the bar and pool tables. Cowboys eager to spend their hard-earned paychecks. And girls from the town hoping they'd spend at least a little on them.

In one corner of the room there was a raised dance floor, ringed by high-top bar tables and stools. The music had been cranked up to a deafening sound, and several couples were already dancing while others were getting up their nerve.

As Ally started past the line of men at the bar, she noted that the waitress was just turning away from her station with a full tray of drinks. If she was going to make her move, now was the time. Taking a deep breath, she charged full-speed ahead. She and the waitress were seconds from colliding when a hand darted out and caught Ally by the arm, dragging her out of the way. The waitress, unaware of what had nearly happened, sailed on past.

Ally had counted on the cowboy coming to her rescue. What she hadn't counted on was being imprisoned between a pair of muscular, jean-clad legs. She looked up to see the cowboy staring down at her with the most charming smile. He was casually straddling the bar stool, one hand resting on his knee, the other still grasping her upper arm with a strength that caught her by surprise.

"Sorry, Red." His voice was low. "Didn't mean to startle you. But I wasn't sure you'd like to find yourself wearing all those drinks."

"Thanks." She reached out a hand to steady herself and came in contact with a chest of solid muscle. Something else she hadn't planned. Even after she moved her hand away and lowered it to her side, she could feel her fingers tingling from the touch of him.

Aware of the intimacy, not to mention the awkwardness of their positions, she took a step back. "I owe you for that." She looked up. "Can I buy you a drink?"

He hadn't been expecting those eyes. Green, with little flecks of gold. Or the reaction he'd felt from that simple touch. Like icy needles down his spine, and then a sudden surge of heat through his veins. "No thanks. I have a beer. Can I buy you one, Red?"

She gritted her teeth at the nickname, but managed to keep her smile in place. "All right."

Ace motioned to the bartender, who placed another long neck in front of him. When he handed it to her, he deliberately allowed his fingers to brush hers, to see if the reaction would be the same.

It was. Only more intense.

Intrigued, he curled his hand around his beer and studied her. He nodded toward the dance floor. "Want to dance?"

She shook her head. "I'm not much for dancing." She glanced toward the pool tables. "Do you play?"

"Now and again."

"I'm learning the game."

He kept himself from grinning. "I noticed. How are you enjoying it so far?"

"It's fun. Of course, it'd be easier if I could just roll the balls into the holes with my hands."

He laughed. "Yeah. It's a lot harder using a stick. But that's the challenge."

She gave him a big, friendly smile. "Want to play one game?"

When he started to shrug his shoulders she added, "Loser can buy the beer."

He shook his head. "I don't want to take your money, Red."

"Oh. I get it." She put a hand on her hip. "Is it because you're so good? Or because I'm so bad?"

"Hey, I didn't mean..." He paused. Then nodded his head reluctantly. "Okay. Come on. One game. Loser buys."

As he trailed her to the tables, Ace reminded himself to take it easy on her. It was obvious that she didn't know the first thing about the game. He didn't want to embarrass her.

It took her almost five minutes to gather up the balls and place them in the rack. Another five to remove it, because they kept rolling apart. Finally she turned to Ace with a shy smile. "You'd better do that thing they do to scatter the balls."

"Break," he reminded her.

"Yeah. That break thing. If I try it, I might miss completely."

With the ease of one who had been doing this for a lifetime he set the cue ball on the opposite end of the table and lined it up, then shot it, scattering the balls. He was good enough to see that none of the balls fell into the pockets. That way, she'd have a fighting chance.

"Your shot, Red."

"Which ones should I aim for?"

"Your call. Since none are in the pocket yet, you can choose."

"I like those little striped balls. I guess I'll aim for them." She picked up a stick and leaned over the table.

"Wait a minute." Ace slid the stick from her hands and turned it around, then handed it back to her. "You use this end to shoot. The other end stays in your hand."

"Oh. Yeah." She gave him a big friendly smile. "Thanks."

As she draped herself over the table, Ace stood back to admire the view.

"Oh, look." She was dancing up and down, though in truth he didn't know why. He'd been so intent on enjoying himself, he'd forgotten to watch her shot. "I got one of those striped balls in the hole."

"Pocket."

"Yeah." She laughed. "So, do I get to play again?"

"Shoot. You get to shoot again."

"Whatever." She turned away and Ace picked up his beer. While she wiggled her way around the table, he pressed the frosty bottle to his temple to cool the heat that was spiralling through him.

"I did it again."

"That's good. Want to try for a third?"

"Can I?"

He grinned. "You keep shooting until you miss. Then it's my turn."

"Oh. All right." She walked around the table, studying the balls, then chose a spot directly in front of him. Leaning over the table, she aimed and missed.

"Oooh. Darn." She picked up her beer and stepped aside.

"That was really good." If not the shot, at least the form was perfect.

Ace cautioned himself not to show off. He dropped two balls and deliberately missed the next.

And so it went. Ace would sink a ball, then force himself to miss his next shot. And though his opponent managed to sink a couple by accident, it was no contest. When the game ended, she gallantly walked to the bar and ordered him a beer.

"How about you?" he asked.

She held hers up. "I haven't finished this one yet."

"Okay." He lifted his, drank. "Thanks, Red." He motioned toward the dance floor. "Ready for that dance yet?"

She shook her head, sending the cloud of red hair dancing around her face and shoulders in the most beguiling way. "Not yet. But I'd really love to learn how you do that break thing."

He shrugged. "Okay." He gathered up the balls and placed them in the triangular rack, setting them up, then motioned for her to come to the opposite end of the table. "As long as you're determined to play, you may as well learn the proper way to hold that stick." He stood behind her and wrapped his arms around her. The minute he did, he realized his mistake. Up close she smelled of something spicy, like a drug that went straight to his head. His heart seemed to fill his chest. He felt as though an entire herd of buffalo was trampling him. It hurt to breathe. And he was so hot, the sweat was beading on his forehead. But it was too late to pull away. Gamely he forced his attention to the position of her hand on the table. "You use this hand to guide the stick. And this one to propel it. Like this." He closed his one hand over hers, then moved her other hand holding the stick. Every movement had him sweating more.

"I see." She turned her face just enough so that her cheek managed to brush his lips.

He could actually feel the flutter of her eyelash against his temple. His heart started racing like a runaway train. The press of her body against his had his entire system working overtime. If he didn't break contact right now, this instant, he was going to embarrass himself in front of everybody in Clancy's.

He released her and took a step back.

"There are a couple of things you want to think about before you break. First of all, you don't want to just scatter the balls."

"I don't?" She looked at him with those big green eyes.

He felt a quick sexual tug and took another step back. "No. You want to consider which balls you want to sink. And you also want to leave as few openings as possible for your opponent."

"You make it sound like a chess game."

"It is, in a way. It's as much strategy as skill. You've got to outthink your opponent."

She pursed her lips. "So much to think about. I'd rather just close my eyes and hope I hit something."

"Yeah. Well. That's fine, as long as you're playing for fun. But if you're playing for money, you can't afford to close your eyes and hope."

"Can we play for money this time?"

He shot her a look. "You just lost and had to buy me a beer. Why would you want to punish yourself again?"

"It's the only way I'll ever really learn this game." She glanced at him, then away. "Unless you think I'm so lousy at this that I'm beyond teaching."

"Hey. I don't think that at all." At her look of disappointment he relented. "Okay. Five bucks."

"Ten," she said. "And I'll let you break. I just know I wouldn't be any good at it."

He was shaking his head as he drove the cue ball into the others, sending them flying. Two balls rolled into the pocket, and he cursed himself for his carelessness. He'd have to be more careful, or he might win by accident.

"Does that mean you get another turn?" she asked softly.

"Yeah." He took aim and deliberately missed the next ball. "Now it's your turn. You're shooting stripes."

"Oh, good. They're the ones I like." She draped herself over the table and took careful aim. When the ball dropped into the pocket she wiggled her whole body like a happy puppy. "I can't believe it. Look. I actually did it."

"Yeah." Ace couldn't help grinning, even though her antics had him sweating again. Even from a distance there was no way to forget the feeling of her body against his. "Now you just have to do it again and again, until the table's empty."

Throughout the game, and the next three that followed, it occurred to Ace that he'd never had this much fun shooting pool. Before, it had always been strictly business. But this was just plain entertainment. He loved watching her. She seemed to speak with her whole body. She chewed her lip, or sometimes stuck out her tongue as she concentrated on a shot. She squinted her eyes, then opened them wide as she made her move. Those wonderful lips would turn down into the most heart-tugging pout when she missed. Whenever she happened to make a lucky shot, her whole face would light up as she danced up and down, or gave him a high five. He was, he realized, having the time of his life. And was feeling more turned on by the game of pool than he'd been in years.

"Here's your money." She slapped down two twenties. "And I owe you a beer."

As she walked away he left the money on the table. When she returned with his beer, she looked at the money, then at him. "What's this?"

"I don't want your money, Red."

"Fair's fair. If we're going to play for money, I intend to pay my debt. Now." She set her beer aside and gathered up the balls. "I think this time I should break."

"Okay." He leaned a hip against the table and watched her, feeling mellow.

"This time I want to play for a hundred."

His head came up. At first he couldn't believe what he'd heard. "What did you...?"

"I said a hundred. It's the only way I can get even, after all these losses." She was smiling. Her lashes fluttered. "Or can't you spare that much?"

"Yeah. Sure I can." He felt a moment's irritation. He didn't mind throwing the game for twenty or thirty dollars. But a hundred? It would be a lot harder to swallow. Still, she was right. She'd been losing all night. If this was what it took for her to walk out feeling good about the evening, what the heck. He reached into his pocket and withdrew a bill.

She set her long neck on top of it and picked up her stick. This time as she leaned over the table, there was a look in her eyes that hadn't been there before. Not so much a look of concentration as a look of determination. Maybe, if his head wasn't feeling quite so fuzzy, and if the music wasn't quite so loud, he'd question it. Instead, he just stood back enjoying the show.

In one clean motion she shot the cue ball, sending the balls scattering. As Ace watched, three striped balls dropped into three separate pockets.

"Well." She turned to him with that dazzling smile. "Looks like it's still my turn."

"Yeah." He watched as she studied the table for a long moment, then sank another ball, and then another.

Ace knew his mouth was hanging open. He couldn't help it. In the blink of an eye, this little female had turned from Sweet Suzie Sunshine into Minnesota Fats. He never even had a chance to make a single shot. When the table was empty she picked up his hundred and stuffed it in the pocket of her jeans, then turned to him with that same warm smile.

"Thanks. You're just about the best teacher I've ever met. Do you believe what I just did?"

"No. I don't." He was studying her with a look of amazement.

"Can we do it again?"

His eyes narrowed. "I don't..."

"Come on. I'll let you break this time."

He knew he wasn't thinking clearly. He knew, also, that a lot of the guys in the crowd had started watching more closely. And some of them had begun making side bets on the outcome.

There was his pride to consider now. His manhood. He had always considered himself king of the pool hustlers. And he was being beaten by an amateur.

"Okay. Double or nothing."

She never even hesitated. "Fine. You break."

He did. And even managed to sink all but two balls. When he missed, his opponent sank them, and demanded another game. And another. With each game, Ace watched the complete transformation of this young woman. Where before her hands had fumbled, they were now steady. Where she had closed her eyes or looked away, she was now completely focused as she took careful aim and sank ball after ball. The only thing that didn't change was that dazzling smile. Especially when she tucked away his last hundred, making his loss an even thousand.

There were snickers from the crowd that had gathered to watch.

She picked up her beer and turned to him with that big, easy smile. "Want to go one more?"

Out of the corner of his eye he saw Cody pushing his way through the crowd until he was beside him.

"Don't know if you've noticed," the old cowboy muttered. "But while she's been buying you beers, she's been nursing that same long neck all night."

As the truth dawned, Ace's eyes narrowed. While he'd allowed himself to become brain-dead, she'd remained stone-cold sober.

It was like a dash of ice water.

"Last chance, cowboy." Her voice was as smooth as velvet. "Double or nothing?"

"No thanks, Red. You've had enough of my hide tonight." Ace placed his stick on the rack and turned away, struggling to cool his heated temper. He couldn't afford a display of fireworks in front of this crowd of regulars.

When he turned back she was already headed toward the door. As he started to follow her he felt Cody's hand on his shoulder. With a muttered oath he brushed it aside and stormed after her. Outside he breathed in the first fresh air he'd inhaled in hours. At once he could feel his head clearing, his mind sharpening. And his temper growing with every step.

Seeing him, she started to run toward a dusty, beat-up truck. She grabbed frantically for the door handle. Before she could yank it open he was beside her, his hand holding the door shut.

In the moonlight it was clear that the smile was gone from her lips. Her eyes were wide with fear. But to her credit, she didn't back down.

"Okay." She fisted her hands on her hips. "So I wasn't some dumb little bimbo who'd never held a pool stick before."

"That's the first honest thing you've said all night." His breath was hot against her cheek as he towered over her. "I have a good notion to turn you upside down and shake every single dollar out of your pockets. I wonder how many other cowboys you suckered tonight?"

"That's none of your business."

"Not my business? A thousand of your dollars belong to me."

"Used to belong to you. They're mine now."

She took a step backward and stumbled. When he reached out to grab her she ducked, then came up swinging, catching him by surprise and sending him sprawling in the dirt. She used that moment to turn and yank open the door before scrambling inside. Eager to escape she turned on the ignition and the old truck coughed and sputtered, then died.

Ace regained his footing and leaned in the open window before she could crank it shut. "Looks like your luck is beginning to fade, Red."

"It's not my luck you're worried about. It's your own. This just wasn't your lucky night, cowboy."

"Luck had nothing to do with what went on in there tonight."

"You need to learn how to accept defeat. Admit it. You could have walked away any time you wanted. Nobody put a gun to your head and made you stay. But I won that money fair and square. And I'm not giving it back."

"Then at least let me know your name and where to find you."

"Yeah. That'll happen." She shot him a grin. "So you can get your revenge?"

"The only revenge I want is on a pool table. I want your word that I can challenge you to another game some time. When I'm sober and feeling lucky."

"When you're feeling stupid, you mean. You can't beat me, cowboy. So don't bother trying. A word of advice. Next time you see me, keep your eyes off my backside and your money in your pocket."

She was so close to the mark, it stung. Though he was humiliated and angry, he reached through the window and gently lifted her chin with his fingertip. Their eyes met and held. At once he felt the quick sexual tug and removed his hand. "You still haven't told me your name, Red."

"Red will do." She turned her attention back to the ignition. This time the old engine sputtered, then caught. She put the truck in gear and the wheels spewed gravel as she took off, leaving Ace to stare after her in frustration.

In the silence that followed he heard Cody's voice beside him in the darkness. "Come on, son. Give me your keys. You're in no shape to drive."

"Yeah. Here." Ace tossed the keys, then, minutes later, as the truck rolled to a stop beside him, he climbed into the passenger side and slumped in the seat.

As they headed along the deserted highway that took them out of town and back to the Double W, Ace stared morosely out the window. Finally he broke the silence. "How did that happen?"

"How? She hustled you, boy."

He turned to study the old man's profile. "Oldest con in the world. And I fell for it. I haven't been suckered like that since I was twelve years old. And it hurts, Cody. It hurts like hell."

They drove for miles, while Ace continued to stare broodingly out the window. Finally he turned. "You think I'm losing my edge?"

Cody grinned. "Hell, son. You're just a man. What chance have you got against a female with all that going for her?"

"Yeah. Who'd have thought? Did you see her, Cody?"

"Yep. She was good."

"Good? How about that time she pretended to look away, and still managed to make her shot? Or the time she sank two balls in a row with the wrong end of the stick?" He pounded his fist into his open palm. "Oh, man was I suckered. How could I have been that blind?"

"'Cause you let her get you drunk."

"Yeah. She is some fine piece of work. I've got to find out her name, Cody."

"That wouldn't be smart, son. Just let it go."

Ace looked away, his pride still wounded, his anger starting to build all over again. "I'm not going to let it go. She owes me. And one way or another I intend to collect."

Chapter 2

"Hey, Ace." The pounding on his bedroom door had Ace lifting his head from beneath his pillow like a wounded grizzly. At the sudden movement his head started throbbing, and morning sunlight stabbed his eyes.

He'd been awake half the night thinking about the redhead who'd made a fool of him. On his own turf. That's what stung the most. The thought of it, of her, had cost him dearly.

The door was thrown open and his brother, Hazard, paused in the doorway. "Cass is on the phone. Wants to know why you missed your nine o'clock appointment with that government guy."

"Government...?" Ace sat up, his head swimming. "It's nine o'clock already?"

"No. It's nine-thirty. Some Washington guy's been cooling his heels up at WildeMining for half an hour.

Cass doesn't think he'll accept any more coffee and doughnuts. Or any more excuses.''

Hazard turned away with a grin as the air turned blue with a stream of oaths. He sauntered into the kitchen and kissed his wife Erin. Then he greeted his brother Chance and sister-in-law Maggie, who was just lifting a platter of steaks and eggs from the stove. ''If that scene in Ace's room was any indication of his mood, we better be ready to duck when our little brother shows his face this morning.''

Chance looked up from his computer, where he'd been getting the latest stock reports. ''Probably couldn't meet any girls at Clancy's last night.'' He glanced at Cody, who had sauntered in from the barn. ''Didn't you go into town with him?''

''Yep.'' The old cowboy took his time hanging his hat at the door, before making his way toward the table.

''Well?'' Hazard took a seat across from him. ''Is that it? Ace is smarting because he couldn't ply his charm on any females?''

''Oh, there were females, all right. One in particular.''

That snagged the attention of Erin and Maggie.

''Was she pretty?'' Maggie hovered, filling Cody's coffee cup.

''Best-looking filly in the place.''

''Are you saying she didn't pay any attention to Ace?'' Erin looked as surprised as the others. Ace's attraction to the opposite sex was legendary.

''Oh, she paid him lots of attention.''

''Then why…?''

They all looked up as Ace dashed into the room, his tie askew, his briefcase trailing the edges of several documents.

"Good morning, Ace." Maggie gave him her sweetest smile. "Sit right down. Breakfast is ready."

"No time. I already called Frank and told him to have the copter standing by. He's not too happy about flying up to the mine with that storm front moving in." He gulped a couple of aspirin and downed a glass of juice while the others merely stared.

"Will you be home for dinner?"

He shrugged. Even that small movement cost him. Then he turned and realized the entire family was watching him. "What? What're you all looking at?"

When they said nothing he glowered at Cody. "You told them, didn't you?"

"Told us what?" Chance looked from Cody to his brother.

When the old man said nothing, Ace let out a long, slow breath. "I got...hustled last night. Out of a thousand bucks."

"You?" Hazard almost swallowed his toast whole.

"Yeah. By a woman."

"A woman?"

Ace nodded. "A woman with the face of an angel and a mind like a steel trap. And hands that could make a pool stick just about dance and sing."

"I don't care if she could make the Statue of Liberty dance and sing." Chance was shaking his head in disbelief. "We're talking about you, Ace. How did you let this happen?"

"I got drunk."

Maggie blinked. "Ace, I've never seen you drink more than two beers in any given night."

"Yeah. I always figure I have to be sharp, in case there's a chance for a game. But the loser had to buy, and she kept losing, and I kept on trying to lose so I wouldn't embarrass her. And the next thing I knew, I was stupid drunk and she was a thousand dollars richer.'' He turned toward the door, then turned back. ''And if you repeat a word of what I've just told you, I'll deny everything. Come on, Cody,'' he snarled. ''Get me out to the helicopter pad.''

When he stormed away, the others around the table remained silent until the door was safely closed. Then they burst into gales of laughter.

''I wish I'd been there.'' Chance stood and began to pace. ''Oh, how I wish I'd seen that.'' He shook his head. ''Can you just imagine Ace's reaction when he realized he'd been conned?''

''After all these years of being the world's best.'' Hazard helped himself to more steak and eggs. ''I sure would love to meet the female who beat my little brother.''

''Yeah.'' Chance grinned at his wife. ''And I'd hate to be in her shoes if he ever runs into her again.''

''Ace.'' As soon as he stepped through the door of his outer office, Cass cornered him. ''Before you greet Curtis, I want you to meet my replacement.''

''That can wait. Curtis can't.''

''But there's so little time left…''

Before Cass could say more he yanked open the door.

''Mr. Curtis.'' Ace breezed through the open doorway, wearing his best pool-hustler smile, his hand extended.

''There's nothing I hate more than to be left twiddling my thumbs over a missed appointment.'' Phillip Curtis had the manner and bearing of a military general. White hair cut razor-sharp. Dark suit neatly pressed. Shoes polished to a high shine. A conservative tie that his father might have owned twenty years earlier.

"I'm really sorry about this delay. A…family matter. Couldn't be helped."

"I didn't know you were married."

"I'm not. I was talking about…my two brothers and their wives. You met them when you had dinner at the Double W."

"One of your family is ill?"

"Yes. Unfortunately." He didn't bother to relate which one. But he didn't consider it a lie, since he was feeling far from healthy at the moment. In fact, a headache still throbbed behind his temples.

"Sorry. But wasted time is wasted money, in my opinion. Don't know about your time, Wilde, but mine is too valuable to waste."

"I quite agree. So, in order to save some of our precious time, I have my driver standing by to take us directly to the mine."

"I've already toured your mine, Mr. Wilde."

"I know that. But I think you'll be interested in a couple of innovations that have recently been installed." Ace winked at Cass and smoothly steered the man toward the exit. "We're not only going to be on time with our delivery to the government, we'll actually beat the timetable we established earlier."

"You'll put that in writing?"

Ace punched the elevator button. "If you'd like an addendum to the contract. But as long as you're happy with the delivery schedule we originally agreed upon…" He waited until Curtis preceded him, then punched the buttons and watched as the doors glided silently closed. "…It seems unnecessary to change

them now. I'll just give you my word that we'll meet
or beat every deadline in that contract.''

''I don't put any faith in handshake agreements,
Wilde. If a man's as good as his word, let him write it
down and sign it.''

Ace sighed. Even on his best day, he didn't look
forward to dealing with Phillip Curtis. The man always
gave him a headache. Today, it was threatening to become a migraine.

WildeMining was an impressive sight. A modern
chrome-and-glass facility stood at the center. This
housed the offices and the computer-generated system
that could locate, in the blink of a cursor, any malfunction in equipment. Around this nerve center, like
spokes in a wheel, were the paved roads leading to and
from the various mines themselves. These roads
hummed day and night with trucks hauling coal, gravel,
or precious uranium for government consumption.

Each mine had a separate set of buildings containing
its own cafeteria, medical center and lounge where
workers could relax between shifts.

Years earlier Ace had given his word to his brother
Hazard that the operation of the mines would never
threaten the Double W land or animals. To that end the
mines were located as far as possible from the range
land, on the northernmost boundary between Wyoming
and Montana, spanning almost twenty miles of once-
isolated property. It made traveling to and from work
a difficult venture for Ace, who often relied on the
family helicopter for transportation. Without it he was
forced to use up precious hours in drive time.

For the next three hours Ace gave Phillip Curtis the
grand tour, determined to make up for his morning's
lapse.

''I'm really proud of this facility.'' He pointed to the employees who continuously studied the series of wall-mounted monitors around the control room. ''Our mines are lined with a system of video cameras that allow us to see everything as it happens. There isn't a man or a machine that can't be located at the push of a button.''

Curtis watched while one of the attendants carried on a conversation with a manager deep inside the mine. When the manager complained about the malfunction of a piece of equipment, the attendant was able to bring the image up on the screen, where the problem was quickly diagnosed, and the proper part dispatched.

Phillip Curtis turned to Ace. ''Very impressive, Wilde.''

Pleased, Ace nodded. A short time later he was standing on the helicopter pad, shaking hands with a satisfied client.

''I'll expect that amended contract to be on my desk when I arrive back in Washington.''

''Don't worry. It'll be there.'' Ace kept his smile in place as Curtis stepped aboard and settled himself in his seat. ''And I'm sorry again about the delay this morning.''

He waved as the copter lifted into the air. Then, desperately in need of aspirin, he turned and made his way back to his office where he sat down and punched a button on his desk.

''Cass.''

There was no response.

He swore and made his way out to her desk. It was empty. As was the outer office, where the receptionist usually sat. Out of the corner of his eye he caught sight of a woman's tan skirt as she rounded a corner on her way toward the women's lounge.

He glanced around in frustration. Finding nobody to help, he began rummaging through the drawers of his assistant's desk. He came up empty-handed and swore again.

Seeing one of the young women from the office just about to step onto the elevator he stopped her. "Where is everybody, Marla?"

She seemed surprised by the question. "They're down in the cafeteria, Mr. Wilde. Saying goodbye to Cass. I figured you were already there. Aren't you supposed to make the presentation of our gift?"

"Oh. Yeah." He turned away, mentally cursing himself. How many more things could he forget in the course of a single day?

He stormed into his office and opened a cabinet. Inside was a beautifully wrapped package which the office staff had given him more than a week ago. Beside it was the card he'd chosen for Cass. Carrying both, he headed toward the cafeteria.

Inside, the noise level was deafening. The employees from accounting were making a presentation of their gift, along with a bawdy poem about Cass Kellerman and her husband-to-be. It brought down the house.

Cass, with her usual dimpled smile, accepted graciously, then made a few off-color comments of her own, which had them laughing even louder.

She looked up when she caught sight of Ace. "Well. Finally our boss is here. I was afraid he might have to accompany our Washington guest all the way back home on bended knee to save his...contract."

Ace stepped forward. On his face was the famous Wilde grin. "It's okay, Cass. You can tell the truth.

It's my hide I needed to save, along with the contract. And believe me, our Washington guest tore a couple of strips off my hide. But other than that, I'm still standing.''

She stared pointedly at the gift. ''Is that mine? Or are you going to hog it?''

''It's for you.'' He continued holding it. ''But before I hand it over, I have to read you the note that goes with it.''

In a loud voice he read the sentimental note written by the women in the office. When he was through, he saw Cass blink away a tear before tearing open the wrappings. Inside was a set of goblets, champagne flutes and water glasses, all bearing the imprint of elegant crystal.

Amid the oohs and aahs, Ace said dryly, ''Now that's what every ranch in Wyoming needs. Good crystal.''

''Don't knock it.'' Cass pursed her lips. ''Or when you come by for a visit, I'll serve you a drink in an old Mason jar.''

The others laughed, enjoying the easy banter between Cass and her boss.

''Oh.'' As an afterthought, he handed her an envelope. ''And this is from me.''

She read the handwritten card and her eyes misted again. Then she looked at the amount of the check enclosed and her jaw dropped. ''Are you serious, Ace? Is this all for me?''

''Yeah.'' He grinned. ''And if you're smart, you won't mention it to Larry. That'll be your mad money in case it doesn't work out.''

''Oh, you.'' She slapped his arm good-naturedly, before taking a second look at the check and then hugging him fiercely.

Two of the women from the office came forward with a cake, and Cass admired it before cutting it into slices and passing it around.

When she offered one to Ace he shook his head.

"You're passing up dessert?" She put a hand to his forehead in mock distress. "Are you sick?"

"Yeah. As a matter of fact…" He lowered his voice. "You wouldn't happen to have any aspirin, would you?"

She shook her head. "Not on me. But I can get you some."

She turned away and spoke with one of the women, who hurried from the room. Minutes later the woman returned and held out a bottle.

Cass shook a couple of tablets into Ace's palm and handed him a glass of punch. "This ought to help."

"Thanks, Cass." He gulped the aspirin and drained the glass of punch, watching as the others gathered up the remains of their party and began heading back to their offices. "Want me to carry some of these gifts to your car?"

"Thanks." She piled his arms with boxes, then picked up what was left and led the way.

Outside she opened the trunk of her car and carefully removed the boxes from his grasp. When she closed the lid of the trunk, she turned. "Well. I guess that's it, then."

"It?"

At his blank look she laughed. "I don't know where you went last night, or who you were with, but that must have been some date."

"I don't know what you're talking about."

"I'm talking about the fact that you haven't managed to get one thing right today, Ace. Your nine o'clock appointment with Curtis. My goodbye lunch, which you almost missed completely. And now you've forgotten that I asked to end my last day right after the luncheon party, so Larry and I could fly up to my parents' place in time for the rehearsal tonight."

"Oh, yeah. Right. I haven't forgotten."

"Liar." She shook her head in mock disgust.

"Wait a minute." It suddenly dawned on him. "You can't leave yet. You never even introduced me to your replacement."

"I tried to do that this morning, remember? But you were too busy trying to dazzle old Curtis."

"Come on, Cass." He caught her hand and started dragging her toward the door. "At least handle the introductions before you go."

"Okay."

As they walked inside and rode the elevator, Ace asked, "Was she at your luncheon?"

Cass shook her head. "She volunteered to stay and man the telephones while we partied. I thought that was awfully sweet of her."

They stepped off the elevator and Ace trailed Cass into his office.

As he walked to his desk, Cass reached over and pressed a button. "Allison?"

A voice as smooth as velvet answered. "Yes?"

"Could you please step in here and meet your boss?"

A moment later the door opened and Ace looked up with a smile.

"Allison Brady, I'd like you to meet the guy who'll be signing your paychecks. This is Ace Wilde. Ace, this is Allison. Although she asks that you call her Ally.''

Ace's smile faded as he caught sight of the woman in the doorway. Despite the fact that her hair was pulled back into an elegant twist, nothing could hide the fact that it was the color of flame. And though she was wearing a trim tan suit and simple pumps, she could do nothing to camouflage the long legs and lush body.

His eyes turned to frost. And his voice, when he finally found it, was pure ice.

''Allison Brady.''

The voice he remembered from the night before said simply, ''You're...Ace Wilde?''

Cass turned from Ace to the woman who had remained motionless in the doorway. ''Well, if you two will excuse me, I have a plane to catch.''

She hurried from the room. Leaving the two of them staring at each other in stunned surprise.

Ally knew she needed to say something. But she was convinced that nothing she said now could ever make things right between them.

How could she have possibly made such a stupid blunder? Of all the guys in the world to con, why did she have to pick this one?

Who would have expected the millionaire owner of WildeMining to dress like a cowboy and hang out in a run-down saloon in the middle of nowhere?

''Well I...'' She started to back up. ''I guess I'd better clean out my desk and head out of here.''

As she turned away she heard his voice, thick with anger. ''What's that supposed to mean?''

She stopped. Glanced over her shoulder. He was still

standing at his desk, his hands clenched at his sides, his eyes as dark as thunderclouds. "You certainly don't want me working for you. Not after..." She licked her lips. "Not after last night."

"True enough. But it doesn't look like I have any choice at the moment. Cass is gone. And I have some additions I need written into an important government contract right away." He came around the desk and fixed her with a look. "You do know how to type, don't you?"

She drew herself up stiffly. "If you have any question about my office skills, you can look over the evaluation Cass left. I believe it's there on your desk."

He turned and picked up the three-page document, reading quickly while the woman he was reading about stood perfectly still, watching him. It occurred to Ace that if he hadn't seen her in action the previous night, he'd actually believe all these glowing tributes. The fact that the final page bore Cassidy Kellerman's signature came as a jolt. He'd thought, for a moment, that he was reading a flattering self-analysis, written by Allison Brady herself.

"All right. According to this, you've mastered every office machine ever invented, can type a hundred words a minute, you're a whiz at the computer, and you've all but sprouted wings." He looked up in time to see the little sparks that flared in her eyes. But to her credit, she held her silence. "I already know that last is a lie. Let's see if any of it is true." He sat down and switched on his desktop computer. "I'm going to call up the last contract we signed with the government. I'll make the necessary changes, then I'll expect you to add them in some coherent manner and have them printed and ready for signature before you leave here at five o'clock,'' and he added, ''I'll remind you that the government contracts are top secret. Nobody sees them except me, and those I designate. And since Cass is gone, that just leaves you. For the moment.''

''And when I finish with the contract, then what?'' She hesitated in the doorway.

''And then, Red...'' He emphasized the nickname in a tone of voice that left her no doubt of his feelings, ''I'm sure we'd both be a whole lot more comfortable if you found employment somewhere else.''

She nodded stiffly before walking away.

Chapter 3

Ally turned on the computer and accessed the file. Despite the excessive number of pages, the contract between WildeMining and the government seemed to be pretty basic. It took only a matter of a few hours to clean up the changes, check for typos, and print out a final copy in triplicate. When it was printed, she took a deep breath before stepping into Ace's office.

He was on the speakerphone with a client. He'd removed his suit jacket and tie and rolled the sleeves of his white shirt. Without the formal clothes, he looked more like the cowboy she'd encountered in Clancy's.

The moment she entered, she saw his eyes narrow before he continued his conversation.

"It's true that WildeMining has acquired an interest in Azure Mines. I've already sent one of my foremen, Hank Richards, and a crew to West Virginia to evaluate how much work is needed to get the mine up and run-

ning again. But we're not ready at this time to make
any promises.''

He watched as Ally crossed the room. Up close he
caught the faintest whiff of something spicy and sexy
as hell. Completely at odds with that business suit and
sensible shoes. As she bent to place copies of the contract on his desk he found himself staring at the darkened cleft beneath the neckline of the plain white
blouse. He could still remember the lush body she'd
been so eager to display last night.

From this distance he could see that she wasn't at
all as cool as she'd first appeared. A little pulse-beat
fluttered at her throat, indicating nerves. That discovery
gave him a perverse sense of satisfaction.

He flicked a glance over her, then continued in that
same tone. ''But I will promise you this, Mr. Sex...''
He paused. Cursed himself. ''Mr. Saxton. When the
mine is ready to run at full capacity, you'll be the first
one I contact.''

He disconnected, then stared at Ally's retreating
back. She was a distraction. A definite distraction. But
it had nothing to do with the way she looked, all cool
and efficient in proper business clothes. It was a purely
gut reaction, because he couldn't forget about the way
she'd fleeced him at Clancy's.

Without a word he picked up the contract and read
it carefully. Satisfied, he buzzed her and waited until
she paused in the doorway.

''Yes?''

That same voice. Smooth as aged bourbon. The kind
of voice, he thought, that whispered over a man's
senses and had him thinking about things better left
alone. ''Okay, Red. I've proofed the contract and
signed it.'' He held out the pile of pages. ''You can

send two copies by overnight mail to Phillip Curtis in Washington. File the third copy in our government file.''

She accepted the documents from his hand and turned away. He watched the sway of her hips and remembered the way she'd looked in those skintight jeans and that little-bit-of-a-shirt. Seeing her now it was hard to believe she was the same woman.

But she was, he reminded himself. The same con artist. Only now she was posing as a cool and competent office assistant.

A short time later he paused in the doorway of his office, noting with satisfaction that his new ex-assistant was busy packing up her meager belongings. A photo. A notebook. A few pens. Not enough to fill the leather briefcase she lifted from the desktop.

She looked up, then away, avoiding his eyes. ''The courier just left. The contracts are on their way.'' She took a breath. ''I expect to be paid for the work I did here this past week.''

''Don't worry.'' He gave a thin smile. ''The check will be in the mail. As soon as I find someone to replace you.''

She turned away, pulling the strap over her shoulder. A minute later he heard the bell signaling the arrival of the elevator. And then there was only silence.

He returned to his office and walked to the window to watch as she emerged minutes later and walked toward her dusty truck in the employee parking area. It took several minutes before she drove away, and Ace realized she'd probably been forced to try the engine several times before it started.

He walked back to his desk and, seeing his hand-written notes, decided to file them along with the contract. He walked to his assistant's office and unlocked the government file cabinet. When he found the proper folder, he lifted it out of the drawer and began affixing the notes with a paper clip. As he did, his glance fell on the words of the second paragraph. What was this? He hadn't authorized this change. Alarmed, he started reading more. Before he'd even completed the first page he found another glaring error. His annoyance was quickly becoming panic. He read further, and discovered several more. By the time he finished reading, he was rigid with fury. All in all he'd counted five errors. Each one would cost the company, not only in loss of prestige, but in millions of dollars.

With a string of oaths he dashed out of his office and stared around. The outer office was empty. All the employees had left for the day.

He returned to his office and began phoning overnight carriers, frantic to determine which one had picked up the contract. When he finally located the one that was delivering the documents, it took another series of calls to the carrier's dispatcher before he could be assured that the mail would be returned to WildeMining by morning.

Phillip Curtis would be furious when the contracts weren't on his desk in Washington. But that was the least of Ace's worries at the moment.

He went through Cass's desk until he located the address of Allison Brady. Then he phoned one of the mine managers.

"Kent. It's Ace. Can you bring one of the mine trucks to my office right away?" He listened. Nodded. "Thanks. I'll be out front waiting."

Minutes later he got behind the wheel of the pickup truck and took off in a cloud of dust. There was a good chance that the address in the file was a phony, and that Allison Brady was probably long gone by now. She'd be a fool to stick around. Someone must have paid her handsomely to sabotage this deal. And since she had a good hour headstart, he'd be lucky to find more than her dust.

Still, he had to give it a try. If he found her, he'd personally throttle her within an inch of her life. Then he'd gladly turn her over to the authorities. Altering government documents ought to buy her a little time behind bars.

"Nobody deserves it more, Red," he muttered as he turned onto the dusty one-lane road that seemed to lead to nowhere. She wasn't guilty of a simple pool-hustle now. This was serious business.

Ace had been driving for miles along this narrow, rutted dirt track. Daylight was quickly fading behind a solid wall of storm clouds that billowed overhead.

His first guess was probably correct. The address was a phony. But here and there he saw scrawny cattle grazing on dried patches of range grass. And in the distance he could make out what appeared to be a ranch house and some outbuildings. None of the Double W's herds or range shacks were in this area. The closest was miles from here.

As he drew near his eyes narrowed with disbelief. Up ahead was a shabby ranch house. From the looks of it, someone was living here. Living smack in the middle of Wilde property.

His temper went up another notch as he remembered. From the time he'd been a kid he'd heard the stories about Harlan Brady, a crazy old coot who'd refused to sell his hardscrabble strip of land, even though Wes

Wilde had offered him twice what it was worth. To
this day the old man lived out here all alone, thumbing
his nose at civilization. Ace shook his head. Harlan
Brady. And then another thought struck. Brady. Allison
Brady. If he hadn't driven out here, he might never
have made the connection.

If she was related to Harlan Brady, it wouldn't have
taken money to get her to do whatever she could to
ruin the Wildes. She'd have done it just for spite. To
even the score for some feud that had erupted a generation ago.

He rolled to a stop and stepped down from the truck.
The wind had picked up, whipping his hair about
wildly. Out of the corner of his eye he saw a streak of
yellow, seconds before a big shaggy dog came running
at him, teeth bared. Behind him was a little brown-and-
white mutt that kept up a steady barking.

"Hello, old fellow." Ace stood perfectly still and
held out his hand.

The yellow dog sniffed and watched him, but made
no attempt to come close.

The door slammed and Ace looked up to see Allison
standing on the rickety porch. She had changed into
faded jeans and a shirt with the sleeves rolled to her
elbows. Her hair was pulled back in a ponytail.

She lifted a hand to drag a lock of hair out of her
eyes. "What're you doing here?"

"I came to talk to you."

"What about?"

He took a step toward her and the yellow dog
growled a warning low in its throat.

Ace glanced from her to the dog. "Think you could
call off your attack dog first?"

"I'm not so sure that's wise." She paused a moment, then said grudgingly, "Buster. Good dog. Come."

The yellow dog moved away to stand beside her. Behind him, the little yapper fell silent and followed suit.

"All right. What do you want to talk to me about?"

"This." He walked up to her and held out the contract.

She flicked a glance over it. "What about it?"

He was watching her face, hoping to see some change in her expression. He was almost disappointed to see none. She was a better actress than he'd anticipated.

"Read the first page."

With a puzzled look she began to read. Suddenly her head came up. "Why did you make these changes?"

"I didn't. You did. And I came here to find out why."

She shook her head and handed him back the paper. "I typed that contract exactly as you wanted it. You ought to know that. You proofed it before I contacted the carrier."

He tried to keep the anger from his voice, but it wasn't possible. "There was plenty of time for you to make these changes before the carrier arrived."

"I just told you. I didn't make those changes."

"Then who did?"

She gave a sigh of impatience. "I don't know. And furthermore, I don't care. In case you've forgotten, I don't work for you anymore. You fired me." She started to turn away.

Stung by her attitude he grabbed her by the shoulder. At once the yellow dog leapt up and closed its jaws around Ace's hand.

Hearing the snarl, followed by a string of oaths, Allison whirled and called frantically, "Down, Buster. Down, boy."

It took no more than her shouted command to have the dog release its hold on him. She lifted Ace's hand for her inspection. "The skin's been broken, but it doesn't look too serious. Still, you're bleeding. Come inside."

He yanked his hand free, annoyed by the sizzle that had raced up his arm like an electric current the moment she'd touched him. "Look. Forget about the blood. What I want to know is why you altered this document. Were you paid to do this? Or was it just because of who I am?"

For a moment he thought he saw fire streaking out of those green eyes. Then they frosted over and her voice was pure ice. "I don't intend to say this again. I never made those changes. If you didn't authorize them, you'd better take a close look at the rest of your employees." Seeing blood dripping from his hand she held the door. "Anything else you have to say you can say inside while I get that bleeding stopped."

Because his hand was beginning to burn like the fires of hell, he followed her inside. He paused and looked around in surprise. He'd expected it to look as tired and shabby as the outside. Instead, it looked inviting. Colorful rugs had been tossed artfully over gleaming hardwood floors. The furniture was a comfortable mix of Western antiques with a few contemporary pieces. An ancient rolltop desk sat against one wall. Beside it was a black, high-back leather chair. A stone fireplace dominated one wall, soaring up two stories. Along the far upper wall was a gallery that ran the length of the house. An ornate leather-and-silver saddle had been tossed over the balcony. Directly below the gallery was a pool table, with an exquisite silver lamp hanging above it.

With the two dogs trailing behind, Allison led Ace through the great room into a big open kitchen, where a streak of lightning was clearly illuminated through the skylights. Here were more surprises. The cabinets were mountain ash and appeared to be hand-hewn and very old. The countertops were Spanish tile. The table had been set in a large bay window. The base of the table consisted of a giant boulder on which had been placed a circle of glass. The chairs looked as old as the original structure. Seat cushions had been added, giving the room a splash of color. Beyond the windows the occasional flashes of lightning revealed a patio, with tables and chairs and a charcoal grill set atop a stone fire pit.

Allison turned on the kitchen taps. "Here. Let's get this blood first."

She plunged Ace's hand under the water and scrubbed. His fingers, she noted, weren't soft like a businessman's. They were hard and calloused like those of a rancher or a man who worked with his hands. That realization came as a surprise.

He sucked in a breath as she poured disinfectant over the cuts, then wrapped the hand with strips of gauze.

"Sorry if this hurts." She could feel him watching her as she worked.

"No, you're not."

She looked up. Shrugged. "You're right. I'm not sorry."

He struggled to ignore the pleasant sensations he experienced with every touch, and reminded himself why he was here. "Now about that contract. It could only be altered from my computer or yours. The other computers in the office don't have access.''

When she said nothing more in her defense he ran a hand through his hair in frustration. ''All right. Since you insist that you didn't make these changes, tell me this. Did you leave your desk from the time you printed out these contracts until the carrier arrived?''

She thought a moment, then said, ''Yes. Cass had left a list of instructions on my desk. One of them was to check the supply room for printer paper and additional fax paper. I was gone for maybe ten or fifteen minutes.''

''Was your computer on?''

She nodded. ''But when I returned, the completed contracts were lying on top of the mailing envelope just the way I'd left them.'' She looked up. ''But wait. They were already signed. If anyone altered them, what would they do about your signature?''

He hadn't thought about that. He'd been too busy worrying about the errors. He flipped the pages until he came to the last page. Both of them stared at the signature.

Allison looked up at his muttered exclamation. ''It isn't yours?''

He shook his head. ''A pretty good imitation. But that isn't my signature.''

''You're sure?''

''I'm sure.'' He mentally went over every line and curve of his name. Someone had taken a great deal of time learning his distinctive scrawl. Someone who was determined to ruin him. ''Now about your...''

He looked up at the strange sound that seemed to be coming closer. Through the open doorway came an old man seated in an electric scooter. His snowy hair was so long it resembled a lion's mane, sweeping back from a leathery face that was still ruggedly handsome. His eyes were as bright as a child's at Christmas.

"Hoo boy, look at this, Allycat." The voice was a deep rumble of laughter. Though he scraped the doorway as he passed through, and nearly ran over the yellow dog's tail, he seemed not to notice. "I can't believe how I can get around in this."

He came to a screeching halt and looked up in surprise. "What's this? Allycat, you never mentioned you had a fella."

Ally flushed. "Gramps, this isn't a boyfriend. This is my boss, Ace..."

"Boss is it?" The old man's eyes, as green as Allison's, studied Ace with intense, almost childlike, interest. "Name's Harlan Brady. And I'm mighty grateful to you for giving my granddaughter a job that pays so well." He indicated the scooter. "She bought me this with that bonus you gave her."

"Bonus?" Ace glanced at Ally, but she quickly avoided his eyes.

"My little Allycat promised me when she got all those college degrees that she'd come back here to take care of her old gramps." He shook his head. "Truth is, I figured with her good looks she'd find some fella and go off and get herself hitched. But here she is, just like she promised. And the first thing she did was buy me a set of wheels when she found out I'd been housebound." He pressed a button and rode in circles around them. "I've been getting the hang of it all day, and I think I'm getting pretty good. How'm I doing, girl?"

"You're doing fine, Gramps." She waited until he came to a halt before pressing a kiss to his cheek.

He sniffed the air. "Something smells wonderful. What's for supper?"

"Chili. It's all I had time for."

"Great. I love chili." He turned to Ace. "You'll stay for supper. It's the least we can do to thank you for this." He patted his scooter, and before Ace could respond, he started away. "Got some beer somewhere. Allycat, where'd you hide my beer?"

"It's in the fridge, Gramps. But Ace can't stay for supper."

"He can't? Why not?"

"He…has an appointment." She turned to him with a challenging look that dared him to argue. "Don't you, Ace?"

Though it was on the tip of his tongue to agree, he couldn't resist a chance for revenge. Besides, he still wasn't convinced that she was telling the truth. Maybe, with a little more time, he'd catch her in a lie.

Seeing how eager she was to get rid of him, his lips curved in a smile. "I canceled that appointment. I'm free all evening. I'd love to stay for supper."

"Good." Harlan opened the fridge door and held up two cans. "You drink beer, Ace? Or would you rather have whiskey? I got some of that here someplace."

"Beer's fine." Ace stared pointedly at Ally. "Maybe your granddaughter would like to join us."

"Ally doesn't drink."

"She doesn't?" He watched as she turned away. "I'm sure she must have some vices."

"Well." Harlan handed Ace a can of beer and popped the top on his own as he chuckled conspiratorially. "None that she tells me about, anyway."

"That's too bad." Sharing the old man's smile, Ace watched Ally's backside as she stormed around the kitchen, slamming plates and bowls on the table, stirring the chili like it was a witch's brew.

"Why *too bad*?" Harlan took a long pull on his beer and gave a sigh of pleasure.

Ace shrugged. "I just thought it might be fun to find someone who could challenge me to…a game of pool now and then."

"Well, sir, pool's not a vice." Harlan took another sip of beer, then wiped his mouth with the back of his hand. "I consider pool a game of skill and strategy, much like chess."

"Like chess, you say?" Ace had to keep from laughing as Ally paused to glower at him behind the old man's back.

"That's what I told my little Allycat when I taught her the game."

"You taught her to play pool?"

The old man nodded. "When she was just a toddler. She lived with me then. And every night she'd climb up on a stool and shoot ball after ball." He shook his head remembering. "Why, by the time she was five or six, that girl could sink every ball in sequence, without ever missing. You don't ever want to play her for money, son. In no time, she'd own you."

"You don't say?" Ace turned to see the blush that stained Ally's cheeks. It gave him a perverse sense of satisfaction to see her embarrassed. It served her right.

Harlan nodded. "Probably could have put herself through college winning tournaments, if she'd had a mind to."

"How did she put herself through college?"

"Scholarship," the old man said proudly. "My little Allycat was smart as a whip. Still is. I'm sure that's why you hired her, isn't it?"

"Yeah." Ace set his drink aside. He figured it might take him awhile before he enjoyed the taste of beer again. "A man can't have too many smart employees."

"Dinner's ready." Ally set a crock and ladle on a hot pad in the middle of the table.

"Where would you like me to sit?" Ace watched as the old man rolled his scooter to the table.

"Outside might be nice," Ally muttered as she passed him with a salad bowl.

"Right here, Ace." Harlan indicated a chair and Ace waited until Ally sat down before settling himself beside her.

When he saw her shrink back from his touch, he deliberately moved his chair closer.

She passed him the salad bowl and he filled his plate, before passing it to Harlan.

The old man glanced at Ace's hand. "How'd you do that?"

"Buster and I were playing a little rough."

"Dog doesn't know his own strength. Thinks he's still a pup." The old man filled his plate and passed the bowl to his granddaughter.

"Yeah. But I'll know better next time." Ace reached down and scratched the dog behind his ears.

"I wouldn't do that if I were you." Ally nodded toward the two dogs, who were standing guard on either side of her. "As you've already learned, they don't take kindly to strangers."

"Then they won't mind me." He gave her that famous Wilde smile that had melted the hearts of females all across Wyoming. "Now that you've had me to supper, they'll just think of me as one of the family."

"In case you haven't noticed, they're too smart for that."

Ignoring her he touched a hand to the slab of glass. "This is a beautiful table. It looks handmade."

Harlan nodded. "I made it more'n thirty years ago. Used my tractor to roll it into place, then installed the windows around it."

"Why?"

"For the challenge," the old man said simply. "To see if I could do it."

That was something Ace could understand. He'd always loved a challenge. "Is that your trade? Building furniture?"

"Gramps is an artist." Ally's voice revealed her pride. "He built this house, and most of the furniture in it. But his real craft is saddle-making."

"I noticed one on the balcony." At the time he'd thought it looked more like a work of art than a mere saddle.

"Horsemen from all over the world used to commission saddles from Gramps."

Ace turned to him. "I figured you for a rancher, like most of the folks out here."

Harlan shrugged. "I tried my hand at ranching. Figured it would pay the bills during my lean years. But I'm just no good at it."

"Then why do you stay here, if not for the ranching?"

The old man smiled. "It's my land, son. Been in my family for five generations. I get my inspiration from the land. If I lost my land it'd be like…" He looked down. "Like losing the use of my legs all over again." He rubbed a gnarled hand over his knee. "Some kind of degenerative disease, the doctor calls it. Hell, it's nothing but old age. Rheumatism, my father used to call it. Now they give it a fancier name."

"So you grew up here." Ace smoothly changed the subject.

"Yep. Like my father, and his father before him."

"It must have been something, seeing this place before there were people and towns and buildings." With little prodding, Ace drew the old man into talking about the Wyoming of his childhood.

Before long Harlan Brady was regaling them with stories of his misspent youth. "I was a wild kid. Thought nothing of riding horseback clear across Montana and back, carrying nothing but a rifle, and living off the land."

It wasn't until Ace had finished two bowls of chili that he realized just how good it was. And how much fun he was having. By the time he'd polished off a piece of cherry cobbler and a cup of coffee, he was feeling positively mellow. And, he realized, the headache that had plagued him all day was now gone.

After topping off their cups with more coffee, Ally began to clear the table. Without a word Ace helped, stacking the dishes in the sink.

"You don't need to do that." Her words were clipped.

"I know I don't. But you fed me. The least I can do is load the dishwasher." He began rinsing the dishes and placing them on the racks.

Beside him she lowered her voice. "I don't want you helping me. I just want you to leave."

"Yeah." His smile grew. "That's why I'm going to take my sweet time about it."

The more she frowned, the wider grew his smile. It wasn't much, but at least it was some small revenge.

Lightning streaked across the sky, followed by a

deep rumble of thunder. Within minutes rain pelted the windows.

Harlan stifled a yawn. "Storm's been threatening all day. Looks like a mean one. How far you got to drive tonight, Ace?"

"Couple of hours."

"Maybe you ought to spend the night."

"No." Ally's head came up. The word slipped from her lips before she had time to think. She turned away to avoid looking at Ace. "I mean, he couldn't possibly spend the night, Gramps."

"You got a wife and kids expecting you?" the old man asked.

Ace grinned. "I'm not married."

"You see?" Harlan looked pleased as he glanced from his granddaughter to Ace. "Not a night to be on the road. Especially if you've got a far piece to travel."

"I don't mind. I've done it before." Ace dried his hands and glanced at the lightning stabbing the darkness. The helicopter couldn't fly in this weather. He'd be stuck driving the mine truck all the way back to the ranch.

He offered his hand to Harlan. "Thanks for the hospitality, sir. It's much appreciated."

"I enjoyed your company, son. Hope you'll come back soon."

Ace turned to Ally. "Thanks for supper. The chili was great." When she started toward the door he shook his head. "Don't bother to see me out. We'll talk about that…business tomorrow." He was rewarded by twin glints of anger in her eyes.

Before he took a step the two dogs were barring his way. The yellow one was growling.

"Buster. Billy." At a word from Ally the dogs

dropped to their bellies and watched as Ace walked past them and took his leave. It occurred to him as he did, that nothing about this evening had been as he'd expected.

Especially Ally Brady.

Chapter 4

Ace stepped out into the drenching rain and sprinted to his truck. When he opened the door the wind whipped it out of his hand. He climbed inside and had to fight to draw it closed. When he turned the key in the ignition, it made no sound. He tried again and again, then was forced to go out into the rain and lift the hood. After trying for nearly an hour he muttered every rich ripe oath he knew before admitting to himself that the battery was beyond saving. He reached for his cellular phone and punched in a series of numbers. Hearing a voice on the other end he snarled, "Hazard? Ace. I won't be coming home tonight."

He tossed the phone down and slammed the door, then trudged through the rain toward the porch. As he did he noted glumly that most of the lights had been extinguished. Before he even lifted a hand to knock, he could hear the barking inside, followed by sudden light and the sound of approaching footsteps. The door was flung open and he saw the surprise on Ally's face before she composed herself.

"Sorry." He couldn't help staring. She was wearing some sort of clingy kimono that revealed every line and curve of her lush body, making him wonder if she wore anything under it. She'd brushed her hair soft and loose. The effect was as potent as a kick by a mule. "My truck's dead. Looks like I'll have to take your grandfather up on his offer to spend the night."

"You did this deliberately, didn't you?" She stood barring his way, hands on her hips.

"You think I want to spend the night out here?"

She tried to ignore the way he looked, his shirt plastered to his skin, his hands clenched at his sides, eyes blazing with anger. Like a sleek panther ready to strike. "I think you still haven't gotten over that little incident at Clancy's. You want the chance to even the score."

They both looked up at the rumble of Harlan Brady's scooter.

He rolled through the far doorway, his hair mussed, his robe hastily thrown over plaid pajamas. "So, Ace, you've changed your mind about staying the night?"

"Looks that way." Ace moved past Ally and stood dripping water on the floor. "My truck's dead."

"Allycat, don't just stand there. Get the man some towels."

As Ally turned away, she looked as unhappy as Ace felt. Just seeing it lifted his mood considerably. After all, as long as he had to stay here all night, he may as well make her life miserable while he was at it.

"Well, no problem. Ally can drive you in the morning." Harlan watched as his granddaughter returned with a couple of towels. "Good thing you two work together."

"Yes. Isn't it?" she muttered sarcastically.

"Allycat, when he's dried himself, show Ace that spare room upstairs," the old man called.

He waved a hand as he turned his scooter toward the other end of the house. "I'll say good-night now. I'll see you both in the morning."

Ally led Ace through the kitchen to a laundry room. "You can toss your wet things in there. The detergent is in that cupboard." She shot him a challenging look. "You do know how to wash and dry your own things, don't you?"

He merely grinned. The nastier she got, the happier he felt. "Honey, I've been on my own since I was twelve years old. There isn't anything I don't know about taking care of myself."

"I'm not your honey. And I know how the rich live." She indicated the towel. "After you've stripped, start the washer and I'll show you where you can sleep."

As he reached for the buttons of his shirt she turned away.

Seeing her reaction his smile grew. "Maybe you'd like to stay and watch."

"No thanks. You don't have anything that interests me."

"You mean, now that you have my money."

"Look." She turned, only to find that he'd already removed his shirt and was reaching for the buttons at his waist.

She found herself staring at the mat of dark hair on his chest, the ripple of muscles along his arms and shoulders. She hadn't been able to forget what it had felt like to encounter that strength.

At his knowing smile she turned her back and listened to the rustle of clothing as he continued to undress. She waited until she heard him rummaging in the cupboard, and heard the sound of water running, before daring to turn again.

He'd towel-dried his hair. It fell damply over his forehead. He was wearing the towel wrapped loosely at his hips. As he fiddled with the dials of the washer, and hung his suit jacket and pants on a hanger, the muscles of his back and shoulders bunched and tightened. Ally felt a similar tightening deep inside.

He turned and found her watching him. "Okay. I guess you can show me where I'll be sleeping."

Grateful to escape the confines of the small room, she led the way up the stairs. As he passed the saddle, he paused to run a hand over it. The leather was soft as butter. The silver bore an intricate design reminiscent of Arapaho markings Ace had seen on artifacts unearthed at the ranch.

"Nice work."

Ally paused and smiled in spite of herself. "I told you. Gramps is an artist, even though he sees himself as just a guy who makes saddles."

He laughed. "Yeah. And Matisse was just a guy who dabbled in paint."

She seemed surprised. "You know art?"

He shrugged. "A little. Very little. But whenever I've had to fly to Europe with my brother Chance, I usually spend a lot of time in museums while he's wheeling and dealing."

"I would have thought you'd be the one making the deals." She started along the hallway.

He trailed her. "Funny. I thought the same about you."

"Look." She stopped. Turned to face him. "I know you think I ought to apologize for taking your money."

"Taking? Red, it was a hustle. Plain and simple."

"Call it whatever you want." Her eyes were hot again. Hot and fierce. "When I got to the ranch and found that Gramps had become a prisoner in his own home, I was desperate to help him. I found the offer of an electric scooter on the Internet, and ordered it. Then I had to find a way to pay for it."

"And you just happened to find me."

"Yes. And do you know why I picked you for the mark?"

He waited, enjoying the flash and sizzle in those green eyes. They were almost as furious as the storm raging outside.

"It was your boots."

He blinked. That was the last thing he'd expected to hear. "My boots?"

"Custom-made. Almost as expensive as one of Gramps's saddles. I figured a guy who could afford them could afford to lose his money without being too hurt."

He arched a brow. "You picked me for my boots? You didn't know my name?"

"Do you think I'd have pulled such a con on the guy who was going to be my boss? I never dreamed one of the oh-so-rich Wildes would actually hang out in a dump like Clancy's. I may have been desperate, but I wasn't trying to sabotage my own job. Not after the way Cass raved about it."

He paused. "She raved?"

Ally nodded. "About what a great guy you were to work for. And how much she was going to miss the place and the people when she left. She made it sound

like a dream job that half the employees coveted. And
now…'' She stopped, realizing she'd said too much.

"Now.'' He caught her by the arm when she started
to turn away. "Now you've learned that there are con-
sequences for your actions.''

"I don't know what you…''

"You took my money, Red. You conned me. Now
you owe me. And I've just thought of a perfect way
for me to collect that debt.''

She saw his gaze settle on her mouth and knew that
he was going to kiss her. The quick rush of heat told
her that she wanted him to. Still, she tried to resist.

"I owe you nothing, Ace Wilde. Your money
doesn't give you the right to…''

He dragged her into his arms and covered her mouth
with his, expecting it to be the sort of kiss he'd shared
with dozens of women. Hundreds. His lips moved over
hers with all the skill of a man who knew his way
around women. His eyes open, watching her. His hands
at her shoulders holding her when she tried to pull
away.

But the moment their lips touched, everything
changed. In the space of a heartbeat it happened without warning. Their mouths mated in a kiss that was no
longer smooth and polished, but rough with need. A
kiss that was all heat and flash and speed.

Ace wasn't even aware that he'd driven her back
against the wall, his fingers tangled in her hair, his
body pressed to hers. His lungs filled with the taste of
her. A sweetness that was unexpected. A need that
matched his own.

As he took the kiss deeper, he felt her fingers trailing
the muscles of his arms and shoulders, sending delicious curls of pleasure along his spine. Then she

wrapped her arms around his neck and clung, offering whatever he wanted.

She tasted like sin. He drank her in until his head was spinning and his world was suddenly tilting out of control. Little alarm bells were going off in his mind. He realized that if he wasn't careful, he would cross a line. It had never been his intention to go this far. He'd simply wanted to annoy her while satisfying his own need to kiss her. Now it had become something much different.

He needed to end this. Now. Still, he lingered over her mouth, loving the taste of her, the touch of her body, imprinting itself on his. If he could, he'd go on kissing her like this until they were both drunk from it.

Finally, calling on all his willpower, he lifted his head and stared down at her as though seeing her for the first time. He kept his hands on the wall on either side of her, afraid that if he let go, he might stagger.

"Damn you, Ace Wilde." Her breath was coming hard and fast. "You had no right."

"Yeah." His own breath was none too steady. "I could feel you fighting me every step of the way, Red. That's why your arms were locked around my neck."

She flushed and avoided his eyes, knowing there was nothing she could say in her own behalf. Slapping his arm away she turned. "This is the spare room. The bathroom is down the hall."

When she started away he stopped her with a hand on her arm. She felt the heat all the way to her toes.

"And which room do you sleep in?"

"The one next door." Her eyes narrowed. "Why?"

He grinned. "If I should happen to get up in the

night, I wouldn't want to stumble into the wrong room by mistake.''

''I wouldn't worry about it.'' She pointed at the two dogs who moved like dark shadows behind him. ''I don't think Buster or Billy would let you take more than one step inside before they'd wake the whole household.''

''They didn't seem to mind that I had my hands on you just now.'' He bent down and scratched both dogs' ears. Then he straightened. ''You might be surprised at how quickly I can start to feel like family.''

''To dogs, maybe.'' She kept her tone even, though it was an effort. ''Don't forget to toss your clothes in the dryer when you wake up. We don't have any servants in this house.''

He waited until her door closed. Then he let himself into the guest room. After a cursory glance around at the wall of bookshelves and the hand-carved desk, he crossed to the bed and turned down the blankets. Tossing the towel aside he climbed naked between the covers. His nerves were revved, his mind racing in overdrive. Sleep, he knew, would be a long time coming.

In the next room Ally was too agitated to lie down. Instead she paced. And worried. And thought.

Buster and Billy sat, tails wagging, tongues lolling, as they watched her.

Damn the fates that had brought Ace Wilde into Clancy's. How could she have made such a miscalculation? There had been dozens of cowboys in that bar who would have easily lost twenty here, forty there. If she hadn't been greedy to win all the money in a single night, none of this would have happened. Still, it was done. There was nothing she could do to make it right.

From the beginning, she and Ace Wilde had collided like two comets. She touched a finger to her lips. She was still feeling the effects of the latest collision.

He had a killer smile. Charming as hell. With just a hint of danger. Everything about Ace Wilde was sexy. And that spelled danger. The last thing she needed was to get involved with a Wilde.

So far Gramps didn't know his last name. When he found out who Ace was, she didn't want to be around for the fireworks.

Lightning flashed and raindrops pelted the window. She stared into the darkness. He'd smelled of rain. And tasted all dark and mysterious. She hadn't been prepared for him. He'd rocked her with that kiss. Nearly shattered all her defenses. From now on, she'd have to be more careful.

Not that there'd be a next time. She turned away and tossed aside her kimono on a chair before slipping under the covers. At once the two dogs took up their positions on either side of the bed and settled down to sleep.

Ally listened to the sound of their breathing, wishing she could sleep as easily. But the thought of the man on the other side of that wall had her tossing and turning. And replaying in her mind the way she'd felt when he'd kissed her. Hot and cold at the same time. The sound of her blood rushing through her veins, pounding in her temples. Her heartbeat racing, her mind going blank. And those hands, those wonderful clever hands moving over her until she'd nearly wept with need.

And all in the space of a few breathless moments.

She rolled to the other side and pounded a fist in her pillow. And prayed for sleep.

Sunlight played around the edges of the curtains and trailed a path across the bed where Ally lay sleeping. She awoke to find Buster and Billy sprawled across the foot of the bed.

"At least," she said, stroking their heads, "you guys wait until I'm asleep before you invade my space."

She slipped into her kimono and started down the hall. As she passed the guest room she noted with satisfaction that the door was closed. She stepped into the bathroom, then froze.

Ace was standing at the sink shaving. He caught sight of her reflection in the mirror and grinned. "Hope you don't mind. I found this razor by the sink and figured if it's good enough for those legs, it's good enough for my chin." He wiped away the last of the soap and turned, skimming a look down the length of her. "Have I bothered to tell you you have great legs, Red?"

As she let out a hiss of breath she backed up.

He took a step toward her. "Don't go on my account."

Her eyes narrowed. "Just let me know when you're finished."

"I've got an idea. Why don't we share? You can wash my back and I'll wash yours."

"You're just full of ideas, aren't you. Well, I've got a better one. Hurry up, so you can get out of my house and out of my life."

As she started away he caught her arm. "Know what, Red? I'm starting to like you when you're angry." He dragged her close and she was forced to put a hand to his chest to hold him at bay.

At once her hand tingled from the contact. She looked up to see him smiling down at her. How was it possible that a man who smelled of shaving lotion and mint toothpaste could look so sexy?

"You know what, Ace?" Her tone was laced with sarcasm, to hide the little thrill that shot along her spine. "I'm getting really tired of seeing you in that towel."

"Would you like me to take it off?"

He brought a hand to his waist and she turned and fled down the hall. Over her shoulder she called, "I'll give you five minutes. Then I want the shower. By myself."

The last thing she saw was that famous Wilde grin as the bathroom door closed. Then she heard the sound of water running, and Ace whistling in the shower.

A short time later when she made her way to the kitchen she was greeted by the wonderful fragrance of coffee brewing.

She poked her head inside. "Gramps?"

Instead of her grandfather, she saw Ace, wearing a freshly pressed shirt and slacks, stirring something on the stove. Her grandfather sat at his usual place at the table, wearing a wide smile.

"What's this?"

Ace turned. "I figured it was the least I could do to repay your hospitality. By the way, I found the iron and ironing board. Thanks."

"You iron and cook?"

"A little. Enough to look decent in an emergency, and well enough to hold back starvation."

She peered over his shoulder. Crisp bacon was drain-

ing on a paper towel. He had added bits of onion and
pepper to scrambled eggs. Toast was stacked on a plate.

"I guess you haven't left me anything to do."

"You could set the table."

Without a word she carried dishes and silverware to
the table, setting them on colorful place mats while her
grandfather watched.

"Coffee, Gramps?"

He nodded. "I can't wait. Been smelling that ever
since I got in here. Is it ready?"

"It is." She filled three cups with coffee and set
them on the table, while Ace carried the platters across
the room.

Harlan dug into his meal. "Where'd you learn to
make eggs like this, Ace?"

"From my sister-in-law Maggie. She's married to
my oldest brother, Chance."

"She must be some cook." Harlan closed his eyes
in appreciation.

"She is. She used to own a restaurant in Chicago
before she came to Wyoming."

"Allycat, you have to try this."

At her grandfather's urging, Ally helped herself to
some eggs and bacon. After her first taste she gave a
reluctant nod of her head. "Gramps is right. This is
great. What else can you cook?"

Ace laughed. "Not much, I'm afraid. Although I do
grill a mean steak."

"Just happen to have some in the freezer," Harlan
said between bites. "If you'd like to come back later
and work on your truck, I'll have them thawed."

With a look of annoyance, Ally glanced from her
grandfather to Ace. If she didn't know better, she'd
think these two were conspiring to wear her down.

"Gramps, Ace has better things to do than spend another evening here."

"Well, I do have to get that truck working." Ace sat back, sipping coffee and enjoying the frown on her pretty face. "And it could take hours." He winked at Harlan. "You have those steaks thawed, and I'll do the grilling."

"You got yourself a deal." The old man sat back with a look of smug satisfaction. "As for me, I think I can operate these wheels enough that, if I had a ramp, I'd take myself out of this house today and visit my workroom out in the barn."

"That wouldn't be wise, Gramps." Ally shot him a worried glance. "You haven't had much experience with that scooter yet. And after that storm, the ground will be soft. It's just as well you can't leave the house yet. I think you ought to give it a couple more days of practice before you start exploring."

Ace looked up. "You got a couple of boards out in the barn, sir?"

The old man shrugged. "A few. Why?"

"I could probably fix you a ramp in no time." Ace saw the disgusted look from Ally and merely smiled as he got to his feet. "I'll take a look. See what I can come up with."

Half an hour later they heard pounding on the front porch. When Ally opened the door, Ace was just putting the finishing touches on a crude ramp.

After testing it he nodded. "Not very fancy, but it'll do the trick."

Harlan Brady's face was wreathed in smiles. "I'm mighty grateful, son."

Ally frowned. "I wish you'd reconsider, Gramps."

"Nonsense. I haven't been to the workroom in

months. I'm getting rusty.'' He brushed his lips over his granddaughter's cheek. ''Stop acting like a mother hen. I'll be fine.''

He shook hands with Ace. ''I'll see you tonight. Now it's time I got back to earning my living.'' He pushed the button on the scooter and turned a neat circle, then eased down the ramp.

''Speaking of earning a living...'' Ally glanced at the clock. ''I'd better drive you up to the mine.''

Ace stepped inside. ''All in good time. Right now I'm going to clean up the mess I made in your grandfather's kitchen.''

''I can do that later.''

''I'll do it now.'' He strolled to the kitchen and picked up his dishes before heading to the sink. And while Ally watched helplessly, he loaded the dishwasher, and even helped himself to a second cup of coffee.

''Okay.'' He dried his hands. ''I'll take you up on that ride now.''

Ally went in search of her keys, then led the way to her old dusty truck. After several tries, the engine coughed and wheezed, then began chugging.

As they threaded their way along the rutted lane, Ace studied the barren land dotted here and there with cattle. ''Your grandfather ought to stick to making saddles.''

She bristled at the insult. ''You sound like my father.''

At the tone of her voice he turned to look at her. ''He didn't approve of your grandfather's ranching techniques?''

''That's an understatement. They fought constantly.

After my grandmother died Dad wanted Gramps to sell the land so he could have a stake in his own dream.''

"Which was?"

"Anything but ranching. He hated this place."

"Where is he now?"

She swallowed. "He died ten years ago. On an oil rig in the Atlantic."

"I guess that's about as far from ranching as you can get." His tone softened at the look of pain on her face. "How about your mother?"

"She died this past spring. But she was never really healthy or strong after my dad left us. That was the reason I've been gone so long. I couldn't leave her alone. And she refused to return to the ranch. I don't know what I'd have done without Gramps. When my parents took me from this place, I thought I'd die." She looked around, seeing it through the eyes of love. "I missed it so much. I used to call Gramps and cry on the phone. Each time he'd tell me to be patient. It would all work out in time." She shook her head. "I never doubted that I'd come back here. This was the only place that ever felt like home."

Ace fell silent. This was something he could understand. He'd always felt the same way about the Double W.

As they drove up to the mine, Ally felt the tug around her heart. She'd had such high hopes for this job. A chance to earn enough to make her grandfather comfortable in his old age. Enough to make the necessary repairs on the ranch house. There was no other company in the area that could match the salary offered by WildeMining. But she intended to start looking as soon as she dropped Ace off.

As she brought the truck to a stop, Ace turned to

her. "I've been doing some thinking. I need an assistant. The sooner the better. And you need a job. Maybe we should start over."

He saw the way her eyes widened before she composed herself. "Are you saying you'd forget about Clancy's?"

"Yeah." He grinned, feeling expansive. It never occurred to him to admit that he'd pulled hundreds of that same con himself. After all, there was only so much a guy should reveal about himself.

She was staring at him as though trying to figure him out. "And you'd like me to work for you?"

"That's what I'm saying."

Her smile was quick and dazzling. The smile he remembered from that first night. "I'd really like that, Ace. You won't be sorry."

His eyes narrowed on her. "I hope not. I want you to know, Red, you're not off the hook. I intend to hire a firm to do a thorough investigation. If you have so much as a smudge on that reputation, I'll find out about it."

"Don't you worry about my reputation. From what my grandfather told me about your family, you're the one who ought to be concerned about what an investigator will find. It sounds to me like the Wildes have made plenty of enemies through the years."

"I guess we have. But right now there's only one enemy I'm worried about. And that's the one who's trying to destroy the company I built from the ground up. Whoever he is, he won't get away with it. Whoever messed with those contracts is going to pay."

At the fire in his tone Ally shivered. She'd already had a taste of Ace Wilde's temper. She'd hate to be on the receiving end if that temper ever erupted into violence.

Then she pushed aside all thoughts but one. The day was looking a whole lot brighter. That little incident in Clancy's was behind her. She had a job. And that meant she could begin to make her grandfather's life a little easier.

She wouldn't allow herself to think beyond that. But as she parked the truck and followed Ace inside, a nagging little thought intruded. Though she hated to admit it, part of her excitement was due to this man. A man who was stirring up feelings better left alone.

Chapter 5

"**Y**es, Mr. Curtis." Ace sat at his desk, his shirt-sleeves rolled to the elbows. The remains of his forgotten lunch rested beside his computer. "I know I promised to have the contracts on your desk when you arrived back in Washington. But there was a...glitch."

He glanced up as Ally walked into the room and placed a fresh stack of papers on his desk. He read them quickly and noted with satisfaction that the offensive paragraphs had all been deleted.

While the man's voice droned on, he rolled his eyes and Ally had to stifle a laugh.

"I have the contracts here on my desk, showing the new delivery dates. All that's needed is my signature and they'll be winging their way to you." He paused. Listened. "Of course. Overnight delivery. You'll have them on your desk by morning. I give you my word."

He set his teeth against the lecture he'd anticipated. A lecture about a man's word being his bond. About the business community living up to its promises, especially when the welfare of the entire government was at stake. And a reminder that the government would take whatever action deemed necessary if WildeMining didn't live up to its promises. All delivered in that monotone that recalled, for Ace, memories of his misspent youth, when he'd been reprimanded by his high school coach for everything from oggling girls when he should have had his mind on the game, to rumors of his gambling. He nearly smiled. If the coach had known the half of it...

He ran a hand through his hair in frustration as he realized Phillip Curtis wasn't about to stop now. On a roll, he rambled on incessantly about trust, the weaknesses in today's business leaders, and the fact that he was forced to deal with idiots.

"Can I take this away?" At Ally's whispered question, Ace looked up to see her standing beside his desk.

She indicated the tray of half-eaten lunch. He nodded. As she bent to remove it, his smile returned, and he inhaled the spicy perfume, and watched her shapely backside. At least there was something going right today.

"You're absolutely correct, Mr. Curtis. And again, I do apologize. But I believe we're on track now. That little...glitch has been corrected. The contracts are, as we speak, being signed. You'll have them in hand tomorrow."

He was forced to endure several more remarks, delivered in that same stern tone of voice, before he could hang up.

"Ally." He buzzed her desk, and a moment later she was standing in the doorway of his office.

"These are perfect."

She smiled. "Thanks. I've ordered the courier. And I've prepared the mailing envelope." She carried it to his desk. "I think the best way to handle this is to keep it here with you until it's handed over to the mail carrier."

"Good idea. Is the locksmith finished?"

She nodded and handed him a sealed envelope. "Here are the new keys to the government file."

He opened the envelope and offered one to her. "You and I will have the only keys."

She shook her head. "I don't want a key. Until this is resolved, I think you should keep them."

He nodded. "You're right. If I need something from the file, I'll get it myself."

A short time later Ally returned to his office to announce the arrival of a Mr. Thorpe.

"I've been expecting him. Send him in."

Ace stepped from around his desk and offered his hand to the small, rumpled man who entered. Then he closed the door and the two men settled down to business.

"I know my brother Chance has used Thorpe and Associates in the past, when he's had security problems."

Thorpe nodded.

"This was a major breach of security. A government contract that was altered. If those changes hadn't been caught before reaching Washington, WildeMining would have lost millions of dollars in penalties when we wouldn't have been able to live up to the unauthorized delivery dates. Besides the money, there's the matter of our prestige. Washington would have eliminated us from their list of acceptable suppliers. Millions more would have been lost in future contracts."

"This is serious." Thorpe leaned forward. His staccato voice that still carried the flavor of New York rapped like bullets. "Tell me how many people have access to these contracts."

Ace frowned. "It's set up to be strictly confidential. Only my personal assistant and I have keys to the locked files. Only our two computers can access the files that pertain to the government contracts. But in truth, our security was weak. I have a new assistant, who left the contracts on her desk unattended for a period of maybe fifteen minutes."

"Long enough for a motivated thief to do his dirty work."

"Yeah. That's what I'm thinking."

"Still, a thief would have to learn the password to get into the computer files."

Ace shook his head. "I'm told a good hacker could do it without knowing the password."

Thorpe nodded. "True enough. But just to make it harder, establish a new password that only you and your assistant will know." He lifted a brow. "What about this new assistant? Can you vouch for her honesty?"

Ace shrugged. "I'd like to think so. But right now, I want everyone who works in the offices at Wilde-Mining to be scrutinized." He reached for a stack of papers. "Here are the personnel files."

Thorpe accepted them and offered his hand. "Don't worry, Mr. Wilde. That's what I intend to do. When I'm through, you'll know more about your employees than their mamas."

"Thanks, Thorpe." Ace watched as he left, and let out a long, slow breath of air. Now that he'd taken the first steps, he was feeling more in control. Whoever tried this would be caught eventually. In the meantime, he would take nothing for granted.

Ace poked his head around the corner. Ally was hard at work on the computer, calling up a list of orders he'd requested from the files.

As the printer began spitting out the pages, he leaned a hip against her desk. "It's after five. I hope I don't have to pay you overtime."

She looked up smiling. "Are you in a hurry to go? I can have these orders on your desk in a few minutes."

"No rush. Take your time."

He returned to his office and retired to the rest room where he kept a change of clothes. By the time Ally was placing the printouts on his desk, he was wearing jeans and a T-shirt. The transformation was amazing. In the blink of an eye he had gone from business tycoon to cowboy.

Seeing the way she was staring, he gave her a smile and glanced down. "Yeah. Those infamous boots."

She couldn't help laughing. "Come on. I can see that work's over for the day and you're eager for my taxi service."

She grabbed up her purse and led the way to the elevator. The outer office was already empty. The employee parking lot was deserted, except for Ally's dusty old truck. As usual, it took several attempts before the engine started.

"Maybe when I'm through working on my engine, I'd better have a look at this one."

She shrugged. "You can try. But I doubt that anything can be done for it now. I think it's just old age."

"Better not let your grandfather hear you say that. I

have an idea he doesn't take kindly to any mention of something old being beyond repair.''

She laughed. "He's one tough old bird. When I came back here, I found him dragging himself around with the help of a rolling cart. He'd lean on it and push it around the house. He hadn't been out to his workroom in the barn in months.''

"Wasn't there anyone he could have phoned for help?''

Ally shook her head. "Who would he call? There isn't a neighbor for a hundred miles, except...'' She stopped when she realized what she'd almost said. "Anyway, he'd never give in and admit that he needed anything. There's a stubborn streak in him that's a mile wide.''

Ace gave a short laugh. "Sounds like Agnes.''

"Who's that?''

"Agnes Tallfeather. She's been with us since I was a kid.''

"A maid?''

He laughed. "You'd better never let her hear you call her that. She's more like our self-appointed mother hen. She used to cook for us, before Maggie married Chance. And she still lives with us. She does some cleaning, delivers the chow to the bunkhouse. Watches game shows on television. But she's like your grandfather. Tough as they come. Set in her ways. There's no changing her. Still, she's come to accept Maggie and Erin, my sisters-in-law. But not without a lot of effort on their part. She wasn't about to give up her boys without a fight. She wasn't ready to see any part of our lives or hers change.''

"I'm not sure Gramps will ever accept change.''

Ally turned the truck off the rutted road into the yard and pulled to a stop.

She stepped out to a chorus of barking, and endured a warm, wiggly greeting from Buster and Billy.

"It must be nice to be so loved." Ace leaned against the truck as he watched.

"Yeah." She laughed. "Sometimes they practically love me to death."

Before they'd taken half a dozen steps they looked up at the sound of Harlan's voice from the barn. "Glad you're home, Allycat. Ace, if you need any tools, you'll find them out here. I didn't forget the steaks. They're on the kitchen counter. I'll be another hour or so in my workroom. Then I'll join you two."

Ace looked at Ally. "He sounds happy."

Her delight was evident in her smile. "It's the sheer relief of being able to get back to his work. Now that he has the scooter, and the ramp you fixed him, he can get to his workroom again." She started up the porch steps. "I'm going to change. Like Gramps said, help yourself to whatever tools you need from the barn."

He strolled into the cavernous barn and found an old tractor, a stake truck, and a workbench littered with tools. Selecting what he needed, he made his way to the mine truck and lifted the hood, whistling while he worked.

"Hey, cowboy." Ally walked up to her old truck and watched as Ace tinkered under the hood. "I thought you were going to feed us."

"I am. As soon as I finish…" He tightened down a hose with a clamp, then straightened. "…This last little problem." He climbed into the cab and turned the key in the ignition. The engine started on the first attempt, then began humming.

Ally shook her head. "I don't believe it. I don't think this old truck has sounded that good in twenty years."

"Just needed a little tuning. It ought to hold you for a while. But you might want to bring it over to the Double W some weekend and let Cody have a look at it."

"Cody?"

"Cody Bridger. Been helping us out at the ranch since I was a kid. Cody can do anything. Doctor cows, deliver calves, and even keep all our equipment running."

"Is that who taught you?"

He nodded as he wiped his hands on a rag. "Cody's one of my heroes. A real straight-shooter."

"Is he the one I saw sitting next to you at Clancy's?"

"Yeah."

She blushed. "Then I doubt he'd want to work on my truck. I saw the way he was looking at me when I beat you that last game."

"Cody doesn't hold grudges." Ace grinned. "Especially since he called you the best-looking filly in the place."

"He did?" She couldn't help laughing.

"Yeah. And he was right." Ace turned toward the house. "Now I'd better wash up and get that grill started."

In the kitchen he found not only three steaks, but a variety of fresh vegetables that looked as though they'd just been plucked from a garden. "Did you pick these?"

Ally nodded. "It's pretty much gone to weed. Gramps must have planted it, then got too lame to keep it up. But I found some tomatoes, peppers, beets."

"Good." He headed toward the outdoor patio. "I'll grill them with the steaks."

A few minutes later Ally stepped out into the late evening shadows carrying a bottle of wine. She filled two glasses and offered one to Ace.

He arched a brow. "I thought your grandfather said you didn't drink."

"I don't drink very often. But I think this calls for a celebration. Not only did I get my job back, but my truck is running on all cylinders, and I don't have to cook tonight."

He turned the steaks before taking a sip. "Good choice. I haven't had much interest in beer since a certain female got me drunk at Clancy's."

She looked down. "I thought you were going to forget that."

"Yeah. I am. In about a hundred years." His laughter had her smiling.

They both turned as Harlan Brady rolled his scooter across the patio, trailed by the two dogs.

The old man took a deep breath. "Smells good." He glanced at the wine. "No beer, Ace?"

"I'll just sip this tonight."

"Would you like a beer, Gramps?"

He shook his head. "Not much for wine, but I guess I'll try it."

Ally poured a glass and handed it to him. He sipped. Smiled. Looked up to watch the flight of an eagle. "Nothing like a summer night in Wyoming, is there?"

"No, sir." Ace lifted the steaks onto a platter and set it in the center of the wooden table. "Doesn't last nearly long enough. Maybe that's what makes it so sweet."

"Like youth," the old man said. He studied the way the wine looked in the fading light of evening, then seemed to pull himself back from his dark thoughts. "It was good working today. Didn't know if these old hands could still tan the leather and shape the silver. But I haven't lost my touch."

"I was admiring the saddle upstairs on the rail of the balcony." Ace paused as Ally topped off their glasses. "That's fine workmanship, Harlan."

"Thanks, son. I'm proud of my work. Always have been." He grinned. Sipped. "Wasn't always proud of my ranching skills, though. Left a lot to be desired. I always resented the time the chores took. Time I'd have rather spent in my workroom."

Ace held Ally's chair, then took the seat beside her. "Could you have made a living if you'd have given up the ranching to devote full time to your saddle-making?"

The old man shrugged. "Guess I'll never know. Never had the chance to give it the time I wanted."

"Well, you do now, Gramps." Ally speared a steak and placed it on her grandfather's plate, along with an assortment of grilled vegetables, then passed the platter to Ace.

"What's that supposed to mean?" the old man asked.

"I'll be getting a regular paycheck now. I can pay the bills and take care of the ranch chores, and you'll be free to follow your heart."

He put a gnarled hand over hers. "And what about your heart, Allycat?"

"This place holds my heart. You know that, Gramps."

He shook his head and smiled at Ace across the table. "What am I supposed to do with her?"

"I'd say you ought to just enjoy her company."

"And let her pay my bills?"

Ace shrugged. "If that's what she wants."

"Huh. There was a time when men took care of women, not the other way around."

"Times change, Harlan." Ace met his look.

The old man sliced off a piece of meat and chewed. "Best darned steak I've eaten in a long time. What'd you do to it?"

Ace grinned, knowing the old man was trying to change the subject. "Marinated it. Just the way my sister-in-law taught me. So, am I hired?"

"Careful." Ally winked at her grandfather. "As long as you keep my old truck running, and keep on cooking like this, you may find yourself getting roped into stopping by more often than you'd like."

Harlan polished off his steak and sat back with a look of contentment as he sipped the last of his wine. "You in any hurry to get home, Ace?"

Ace shrugged. "Not particularly. Why?"

The old man merely grinned. "Thought after you two cleaned up here you might like to see my workroom."

Ally's mouth dropped open. But to her credit she managed to keep her tone casual. "Your workroom?"

"That's what I said."

"Well." She picked up his empty plate and her own. "I'll just clear away these dishes and we'll take you up on it."

Ace picked up the rest of the dishes and followed

her. "Come on. I'll give you a hand with these dishes."

"No you won't." She took the dishes from his hands and placed them in the sink. "Right now, before Gramps changes his mind, we're going to take him up on that offer."

He shot her a puzzled look. "Why are you in such a hurry?"

"Because," she said, steering him toward the door, "until now, Gramps has never allowed anyone who wasn't family into his workroom."

"This is really something." Ace moved slowly around the room.

An entire section of the barn had been converted into Harlan Brady's studio. There was a large, airy workroom, which had three walls of shelves holding an assortment of supplies. Leather, smooth as butter, with hand-tooled markings. Lengths of precious metal, some twisted, others bearing the distinctive designs which bore the initials of the artist. There were various needles for sewing the leather and tools for assembling the saddles.

One wall was made of glass, allowing natural light to spill into every corner of the room. Overhead were skylights, spilling strips of moonlight across the wooden floor.

"What's over here?" Ace pointed to a closed door.

"A bedroom and bathroom."

"You sleep out here?"

"Used to." The old man glanced at his granddaughter, then away. "So many nights I'd stay out here until I'd fall asleep at my worktable. Then I'd just drag myself in there and bunk for a couple of hours, before it was time to start my morning chores. The last couple of months, I couldn't get out here to do any work at all. Discovered I had a pretty comfortable bedroom back there at the house. But the truth is, I'd rather sleep here. I like being around the leather and the silver. I like the feel of them. I even like breathing in the smell of them.''

Ally walked over to lay a hand on his shoulder. ''Then why don't you bunk out here again?''

''You wouldn't mind? You'd be all alone up there at the house.''

''I'll have Buster and Billy.''

''Well…'' His glance fell on the dogs, who were watching his every move.

At his hesitation she gave a sigh. ''I see. They miss the workroom, too.''

''Yeah.'' The old man grinned. ''They were happy as pups all day out here. Would you be afraid up at the house alone?''

She shook her head. ''I've been alone a long time, Gramps. The only thing I've ever been afraid of is not being able to come back to Wyoming.'' She pressed her forehead to his. ''Back here to you.''

For a moment neither of them spoke, and Ace felt like an intruder.

''You really wouldn't mind?'' Harlan asked.

She shook her head.

The old man looked as delighted as though she'd just given him the gift of a lifetime. ''Hoo boy.'' He rolled the scooter around in circles. ''I get to sleep in my workroom again. You don't know how I've missed this.'' He turned to Ace. ''Thanks for that bonus, son, that made this possible. And for the gift of that ramp.'' He ran a hand over the scooter, then looked up. ''And thanks for supper, Ace. You're a damned fine cook. Now if you two don't mind, I'd like to get back to my work.''

Ally kissed his cheek. Ace shook his hand and walked out into the darkness beside Ally. At the porch they both turned to look back at the lights in the barn.

Ally shook her head. ''He'll probably work until midnight.''

''I wouldn't worry about it. He looked as happy as a kid at Christmas.''

''Yeah. I noticed.'' She paused. Lowered her voice. ''You really are the first person outside the family that he's ever allowed inside that workroom.'' She shook her head. ''I'd like to know how you managed that.''

His smile was back, causing a hitch around her heart. ''It's my charm.''

''Really? I hadn't noticed.''

''Liar.'' He dragged her close. ''Admit it. I'm getting to you, too.''

''Not a chance, cowboy.''

Maybe it was the joy they'd seen on the old man's face. Or maybe it was merely the magic of the summer night, perfumed with the fragrance of roses and wild honeysuckle. Whatever the reason, when he drew her into his arms she offered no resistance.

He brushed his mouth over hers. The merest touch of lips to lips. The effect was so startling, she couldn't seem to stop herself. Her arms circled his neck, drawing him closer until his body was imprinted on hers. He took the kiss deeper. At once Ally was caught up in a kiss so powerful, she could feel her bones melting. Could actually feel her blood heating up. Could hear her heartbeat pulsing like thunder in her chest. And then she was lost as she gave herself up to the pure pleasure.

Ace pressed her back against the door and fed from her lips. Fed a hunger that he hadn't even known he possessed until he tasted her. And now that he'd tasted, he wanted more. He wanted all. He buried his lips in the little hollow of her throat and breathed her in. The thought of taking her here, now, was nearly overpowering.

"Ally." He wasn't certain if he'd spoken her name aloud, or only thought it. But when she drew back to look up at him, he realized she'd heard him.

"We'd..." He was surprised at how difficult it was to speak. Every word seemed to stick in his throat. "We'd be a lot more comfortable in the house."

"The house?" It took her a moment to come back to earth. When she did, her eyes darkened. "No." What had she been thinking? "You have to go, Ace."

"That's not what your kiss just said."

"I...wasn't thinking straight. Now I am."

She saw his smile, quick and dangerous. "Stop thinking." He ran his hands across her shoulders, down her arms, and lowered his head. "It can get you in all kinds of trouble. Instead, just feel."

She did. And, oh, what feelings as his mouth moved over hers with such skill. As he took her higher, she thought she saw lights flashing in front of her eyes. Or were they merely fireflies?

"You..." Reluctantly, she drew away. "You really have to go now, Ace."

He brushed his lips over hers one last time. "I could come inside and help with the dishes."

"Good try." She managed to smile before stepping back, breaking contact. "But the answer is no."

"You're tough, Red."

"Yeah. One of us has to be. Good night, cowboy."

She turned away and stepped inside, then leaned her forehead against the screen door. As he sprinted off the porch she called, "See you tomorrow."

"Yeah." He walked to the truck and climbed inside. When he started the engine and turned on the headlights, he could see her illuminated in the doorway, still watching him.

As he headed out on the long drive back to the Double W, it occurred to him he was getting in way over his head. Ally Brady was beginning to mean a lot more to him than just an office assistant. A whole lot more. And in light of the trouble he was dealing with right now, that could be dangerous.

Chapter 6

"I'm glad the contracts meet with your approval, Mr. Curtis." Ace glanced up as Ally deposited a stack of papers on his desk before hurrying away. That made at least a dozen times she'd been in his office since the start of the work day, and each time, she'd beat a hasty retreat without making eye contact.

He was definitely getting the cold shoulder, but he couldn't figure out why. And he'd been too busy to find even a minute to talk to her.

But he would. Before the day ended, he vowed, he would. And if he found that she was holding that goodnight kiss against him, he'd remind her that she'd participated as enthusiastically as he.

"I appreciate it, Mr. Curtis. You can expect the first shipment to leave WildeMining early next month." He paused. "You bet. Right. Goodbye."

He disconnected and muttered a savage oath when his phone rang yet again. For the next hour he endured a series of business calls that couldn't wait. Finally, with his desk cleared of paperwork, he went in search of Ally. He felt a sense of frustration when he caught sight of her in the outer office, talking and laughing with several of the other employees. Agitated, he returned to his office and buzzed her desk.

Minutes later she stepped inside. "You wanted to see me?"

An understatement. He wanted to devour her. Instead, he said simply, "Would you mind closing the door?"

She did as he asked, then turned to him questioningly.

"You've been avoiding me."

"Ace..."

"Haven't you?"

She swallowed. Nodded.

"Why?"

"I work for you," she said simply.

"So?"

"This just isn't smart, Ace. We have to see each other all day, every day. If something should happen to...strain our business relationship, we wouldn't be able to work comfortably together."

"You mean, if we should happen to develop a personal relationship?"

She nodded. "I gave it a lot of thought after you left." That wasn't at all an apt description. She'd paced the floor of her room for hours, agonizing over the things she was feeling for him. "I just don't think I should...you should..." She let the words trail off.

He would have laughed except that she was so serious. And looked so sad. "Okay." He stepped from around his desk and walked toward her.

"Okay?" She blinked. This wasn't at all the reaction she'd been expecting. She'd debated the wisdom of sharing her thoughts. And she'd anticipated a dozen different arguments that she'd have to endure from him. For some strange reason she felt oddly deflated that he hadn't been willing to debate the issue at all.

"Sure. Sounds very sensible to me." He moved closer, his eyes staring unblinking into hers. "And everyone who knows me knows I'm the most sensible guy in the world." That bold-faced remark almost had him roaring. There wasn't a sensible bone in his gambler's body. "So if you think we ought to cool it, we will."

"Fine. Well." She steeled herself not to back up as he advanced. "Then I guess there's nothing more to say."

"I guess not." He halted mere inches from her. He itched to touch her. He had to curl his hand into a fist at his side to keep from reaching out and just taking.

She turned away, her hand on the knob. "If there's nothing else…"

"There is."

She turned back.

He shrugged and gave her that boyish grin that always seemed to melt her heart. "I thought maybe you'd like to share a pizza at Clancy's after work."

"Clancy's?" She shook her head. "I could never show my face there again, Ace. I'd be too embarrassed."

"Okay." That's what he'd figured. And that's why he'd suggested it. To throw her off-balance. He gave a negligent shrug of his shoulders. "Is there someplace around here?"

After a moment's hesitation she said, "There's a little bar just over the state line in Montana."

"Do they have pizza that tastes like cardboard?"

She laughed. "No. But they have burgers that are really terrible."

"My kind of place. Want to go there after work?"

She was laughing as she nodded. "I suppose I could be persuaded. But I'll have to drive home first and see that Gramps has something to eat in his workroom."

"All right." Ace glanced at his watch. "It's already past quitting time. You go ahead and see to your grandfather. I'll pick you up at your place. I'll just take a minute to change."

Ally turned away and grabbed her purse as she headed toward the elevator. She was halfway home before she realized that she'd just broken all the promises she'd made to herself last night. After that impassioned speech she'd made to Ace, nothing had changed. In fact, she'd just agreed to a date with him.

She groaned. An honest-to-goodness date. What was happening to her? When she was around Ace Wilde, her mind turned to mush. If she wasn't extremely careful, her resolve might do the same.

In his office, Ace was feeling pretty smug. He hadn't lost that old touch. He'd managed to pull that con so smoothly, Ally Brady hadn't even seen it coming. And now, whether she liked it or not, she was going to spend another evening with him.

"What'll you have?" The waitress was wearing a pair of frayed cutoffs and a T-shirt emblazoned with the bar's logo, a red devil, complete with horns and a pitchfork.

"Two long necks and two burgers."

In the smoky Red Devil Bar, Ace and Ally sat in a booth in a darkened corner where they could watch the action. There were four pool tables, all being used. Most of the players wagered nothing more than a beer, or the cost of the next game. But a few of them slapped tens and twenties down on the table when they lost.

Ace nodded toward the nearest pool table. "Want to play?"

She shook her head.

"Why not? Afraid you'll embarrass me again?"

She winced. "That last time wasn't a fair assessment of your skill, Ace. I got you drunk."

"I got myself drunk." He took her hand in his, playing with her fingers. "So why didn't you come here that night in search of suckers?"

"It was too close to Gramps's place. I wanted to be far enough away that nobody would recognize me. So I drove all the way to Prosperous."

"You had a long drive home that night. I bet you were looking over your shoulder the whole way."

She laughed. "I was. What an awful night. I was really scared."

"You were?" He felt her pulse jump when he caressed her wrist and was pleased that it was his touch that was causing such a reaction. "I'd have never guessed. You looked as cool as an iceberg."

"You know what they say. Never let 'em see you sweat."

"Yeah." He lifted her hand to his mouth and pressed a kiss to the palm. And was delighted to realize she was doing exactly that—sweating.

"Here you are." The waitress set down their beers. "Your burgers will be up in a few minutes." She lifted her tray and hurried off.

As Ace brought the bottle to his mouth, Ally grinned. "Think you can handle it?"

"As long as I have only one." His lips curved in a smile. "I may never enjoy the sheer pleasure of a cold beer again."

They watched as two cowboys leaned over the pool table arguing over the best way to sink the last ball. Finally the first cowboy shot and missed, and the second one did the same.

"They'd be easy pickings," Ace said. "Are you sure you're not a little tempted?"

Ally laughed. "Am I that transparent?"

"Yeah." He studied her. "It's your eyes. Those little points of flame shooting out of them are a dead giveaway."

"Then how come you didn't pick up on that clue the night I hustled you?"

"Because you got me drunk."

"You just told me you got yourself drunk."

He caught her hand and studied her long slender fingers. "Who knows? Maybe I got drunk on those big green eyes of yours. Every time I look into them, I feel my head swim."

Ally was relieved when the waitress interrupted them with their burgers and fries. Every time Ace touched her like that she could feel the little licks of fire along her spine. And could feel her resolve slip another notch.

"You were right," he said after his first bite.

'I was? About what?'

"Absolutely the worst burger I've ever tasted. I think it even has Clancy's pizza beat."

Despite his admission, he managed to finish every

bite. When that was gone he smothered the fries in ketchup and dug in.

Ally nodded toward the pool table. "Now our cowboys are going to play for money. As though that will somehow make them better players."

She and Ace shared a laugh.

"A fool and his money…" The moment the words were out of her mouth she wished she could call them back. But it was too late. Ace was looking at her in a strange way.

Though his features never changed, there was a hint of a challenge in his eyes. "That other table is empty. Let's shoot a game of pool."

As she started to protest he shook his head. "No con. And no fuzzy brains. Just straight-up, no-holds-barred pool."

She held back. "What'll we play for?"

His grin was fast and wicked. "What else? Bragging rights."

"Ace, you don't understand. I'm good."

"Yeah." He laughed. "I won't argue with that. And from what your grandfather says, you may be unbeatable. But I deserve a fair shot. Agreed?"

She gave a reluctant nod. "Okay. I agree. But I warn you. I won't pull any punches. I have no intention of holding back and letting you win just for the sake of that fragile male ego."

"Fragile male ego?" His laugh was deep and rich. "Oh, Red. I wouldn't miss this for the world."

Ally watched as he collected the balls and racked them. "Who's going to break?"

"We'll flip a coin." Ace produced a quarter and said, "Call it."

"Heads." Ally watched as he caught it, and held it

out. Then with a grin she picked up her stick. "Looks like my luck holds."

Ace stood back and watched as she took careful aim and sent the balls scattering. "Maybe you think you're the lucky one, Red. But from where I'm standing, I'd say I'm the lucky guy with the best view."

She smacked his arm. "No muddled brain, remember? Pay attention. I'm about to give you a lesson in shooting pool."

And she did. Ace watched with a smile of pure appreciation as she called her shots and sank each of the balls in sequence.

"Red." He leaned close and brushed a kiss over her cheek. "You are pure poetry in motion."

Ally absorbed the quick little rush of heat and had to steady herself against the table. When she took her next shot, the ball rolled to the very lip of the pocket, but failed to drop.

"What's this? Has the lady lost her edge?" Ace wiggled his brows.

"I ought to complain that you took unfair advantage. That kiss did something to my brain."

"Good. Remind me to kiss you again next game." He picked up his stick and sank the rest of the balls.

"Very smooth." Ally shot him an admiring glance. "You didn't play that way the other night."

"Yeah. Just an off night. Something I drank. But I think I'm back on track." He racked the balls. "Okay. We'll call that first game a draw. We both sank the same number of balls. But since I made the last shot, I get the break this game."

He sent the cue ball racing into the cluster of balls, scattering them and setting them up nicely. After that, he ran the table, never missing a shot.

When he was through, Ally shook her head in admiration. "I don't believe it. That was absolutely beautiful. You really are very good, you know."

"Thank you, ma'am." He looked pleased with himself. "Looks like I get the break again." He made a good break, but failed to sink a single ball.

"Uh-oh." Ally took up her stick. "That's going to cost you, cowboy." She sized up the table, then began making shot after shot without a single miss. When there was only one ball left she batted her lashes at him and said slyly, "I'll bank it off the left side, and sink it here." She touched the tip of her stick to the pocket, then proceeded to make the shot with textbook perfection.

When she turned, Ace was grinning from ear to ear. "Like I said, Red. Pure poetry in motion. Watching you shoot pool is just about the prettiest thing I've ever seen."

"Want to play again?"

He shook his head. "We've each won one. That gives us both bragging rights. I think we'd better quit while we're ahead."

"All right." She shot him a mysterious smile. "Now I'll show you a little trick my grandfather taught me when I was just a kid. I've never seen anyone else manage it." She set a ball in the middle of the table and picked up two pool sticks and the cue ball, then proceeded to walk to a second table, which had just been vacated. Holding one stick in each hand she balanced the cue ball between them and launched it so perfectly it flew from one table to the other, rolled directly toward the waiting ball, and sent it sinking into the left pocket.

Ace couldn't hide his astonishment. "Can you do that every time?"

She laughed. "I've never missed. Well, maybe once or twice. But most times, I can do it on the first try."

"I'm not sure I could even launch a ball that accurately with my hand, let alone using two sticks. That's some trick, Red." He was still shaking his head as he took the sticks from her hand and returned them to the rack.

On the far side of the room, next to the jukebox, was a small dance floor. Motioning toward it, he held out his hand. "Come on. Dance with me."

She put her hand in his and allowed him to lead her toward the far side of the room.

Patsy Cline's haunting voice was warbling about being crazy in love. As the words played through her mind, Ally allowed him to draw her even closer, until her lips were pressed to his throat, and his mouth was buried at the hair of her temple.

It was the sweetest torture of Ace's life, to hold her like this, to move with her like this, to breathe her in until his lungs were filled with the sweet, spicy scent of her. He couldn't recall anything or anyone he'd ever wanted so desperately. He wanted, right this minute, to carry her out into the night and, while the darkness closed around them, to make love with her until they were both sated.

What he settled for was moving slowly around the smoke-filled dance floor, while the music washed over him. She felt so good in his arms. So right. With that lush body brushing his, and her fingers playing with the hair at his neck, and her breath warm against his cheek.

The music changed from Patsy to Garth to Trisha.

But through it all, the same plaintive cry for love came through, casting its spell, until the two of them were barely moving. With their arms around each other, and their bodies swaying gently to the music, they felt as if they were the only two people in the world.

Ace stared down into her eyes. "If we don't get out of here soon, Red, I'm going to make a fool of myself right here in front of everybody."

She sighed. "I'm willing."

"To get out of here? Or to see me make a fool of myself?"

"Well…" She laughed. "Since I've already seen the last, let's go for the first."

He caught her hand and led her out into the night. As soon as they reached his truck he gathered her close, desperate for the taste of her lips. But before he could kiss her they heard the sounds of muttered oaths and looked up to see two drunken cowboys engaged in a knock-down-drag-out fistfight.

"Come on." Frustrated, Ace opened the door and helped her inside, then rounded the truck and climbed in the driver's side.

Minutes later they were heading out of town. For the longest time neither of them spoke. But they kept darting glances at one another. And when Ace reached for Ally's hand, and linked his fingers with hers, she felt the heat begin to rise between them until she could hardly breathe.

By the time her grandfather's ranch came into view, the tension shimmered between them like a living, palpable entity. Amid a chorus of barking Ace pulled to a stop and walked around the truck. As she stepped down, Ally glanced toward the barn. The light was on in her grandfather's workroom.

Without a word they walked to the porch, with the dogs trailing at their heels. Ally bent to pet them. Satisfied, Buster and Billy trotted back to the barn, leaving them alone.

When they climbed the steps, Ally paused at the door.

Before she could say a word Ace's arms were crushing her to him. His mouth was savaging hers. Devouring her. And she was lost in a haze of the most amazing sensations.

"This was all I've wanted." He whispered the words against her lips, then inside her mouth, as he took the kiss deeper. "All night. Just this."

Like a starving man he feasted on her. Devoured her. Drank her in. His big hands framed her face and he stared down into her eyes. His own were hot and fierce. His voice a low growl. "You've done something to me, Red." He pressed kisses to her eyelids, her temple, her cheek. "Ever since you walked into my life, I can't think of anything but you." He nibbled the corner of her mouth, then lower, running quick, nibbling kisses down her throat until she nearly sobbed with the need for more. "You make me crazy, Red. I don't know what time it is. What day it is. And I don't care. I don't care about anything but you. But this."

With lips and teeth and tongue he teased and tormented. And all the while his hands roamed her back, her sides, until his thumbs found her breasts and began to stroke.

She tried to think but it was impossible. All she could do was hold on as he took her higher and higher. She knew that if she but said the word, Ace would take her. Here. Now. And this terrible tension between them could be eased. But in some small part of her mind she could hear the warning. He was Ace Wilde. Her boss. And the son of her grandfather's old enemy.

"Ace." She pushed against him, needing a moment to calm the storm raging inside. "I have to…" She dragged air into her lungs. "We have to…"

"I know what we have to do." He covered her mouth with his and stoked the fire higher.

"No." She pushed away, struggling for the strength she needed. "I need to…go inside now."

"All right." His smile was quick.

"Alone."

He leaned his hands on the door on either side of her head and pressed his forehead to hers. "I was afraid you'd say that."

She touched a hand to his cheek. "One of us has to be sensible."

"That again." He took a deep breath and lifted his head. "I take it I'm not invited to spend the night?"

She shook her head. "Too dangerous. We'd never make it."

"Yeah." His smile was back. "But we'd have a great time."

"I have no doubt." She turned and opened the door.

He leaned in the doorway and took her chin in his hand, brushing his lips over hers. "Come to the Double W tomorrow."

"Why?"

"It's Saturday. It's the only way I'll get to see you. I don't think I could go a whole weekend without my Red fix." Before she could say a word he added, "I'll have Cody take a look at your old truck's engine."

"Will you feed me, too?"

"Oh. So you need to be bribed? Yeah. If that's what it takes, I'll even feed you."

"You've got a deal."

He nodded, then stepped off the porch and strolled to the truck.

As he drove along the deserted stretch of road, he realized that his hands on the wheel were none too steady. And his breathing still hadn't returned to normal.

What the hell was happening to him? No woman had ever had this effect on him. Pure lust, he consoled himself. She was a beautiful woman. It was natural enough to want her.

But there was a nagging little thought that was making him uncomfortable. The things he was feeling for Ally were unlike anything he'd ever felt before. Although he'd only known Allison Brady a few days, he felt as if he'd been waiting all his life for her.

Chapter 7

"Gramps?" Ally poked her head in the doorway of Harlan's workroom. Morning sunlight spilled through the windows and skylights. "I brought you breakfast. And a pot of coffee."

"Ah. My angel." He set aside the length of leather and picked up a mug, holding it out while she filled it. He leaned back and drank. "You sure you're all right with this, Allycat?"

"With what?" She set down his plate.

"My being out here so much. Even sleeping out here. I know it makes more work for you. And it seems pretty ungrateful, since you're so recently returned."

"Don't be silly. I'm just happy to see you finding such enjoyment in your work again."

"Yeah. It's good to get back to it. Those last couple of months…" He shook his head. "When I couldn't make these old legs work anymore, and realized I couldn't get out to the barn and back, I started feeling old and useless.''

"You, Gramps?'' Ally put her arms around his neck and kissed his cheek. "You're the youngest man I know.''

His eyes danced with unconcealed pleasure. "Well, that's how I feel now that you've come home. I just hope you don't mind being all alone in that big old house.''

Her voice lowered with emotion. "For years I was alone in places I didn't want to be. Now that I'm here, I don't mind that I'm in the house and you're out here. We have each other, Gramps. That's all that matters.''

"Yep. You got that right.'' He looked up. "I heard you and Ace come back pretty late last night.''

She grinned. "It couldn't have been too late. The lights were still on in your workroom.''

"Don't let that fool you. Doesn't mean a thing.'' He winked. "Sometimes I fall asleep at my workbench and the lights stay on all night.''

"Maybe I'd better start checking up on you before I go to bed, the way you used to check on me all those years ago.''

"Reverse our roles, you mean? Naw. I'm not ready for that yet. Besides, I've got old Buster and Billy to watch over me.''

The two dogs were busy emptying the bowls of dog food Ally had filled from a sack by the door.

She nodded toward the covered plate she'd set on the workbench. "You'd better get to your breakfast before it gets cold.''

He uncovered his plate to reveal poached eggs and crisp bacon. "You really are an angel, Allycat. This is my favorite.''

"I remember."

As she started out she paused. "I already made your lunch. It's in the refrigerator. And there's a pot of stew you'll have to heat up for supper, if I'm not back in time."

"Where're you going?"

"Ace offered to work on the truck engine."

"Now I know why I like that young man. Let's see if he can't keep it running for another couple of years." He smiled. "Don't hurry home."

"Why?" She paused. "Do you have a lady friend coming over?"

"How I wish." He shook his head. "It's been too long. But I can still remember what it was like to be your age. Time just disappears when you're with someone who's good for you. And I think Ace is good for you, Allycat."

She waved and hurried to her truck. As she drove away, she struggled to put aside the guilt that was gnawing at her. She hadn't exactly lied to her grandfather. But, knowing how he felt about the Wildes, she hadn't been truthful either. Still, she consoled herself, there was no point in inviting trouble. Maybe he'd never have to find out just who Ace really was.

Ally drove slowly up the long, winding road that led to the Wilde house. She'd never been here before. Had never even been close to the place that was the closest thing to a mansion in these parts.

As the house came into view she let out a long, slow breath. It was even bigger than she'd imagined. Made of stone and gray-weathered wood, it soared to three stories. Despite the additions of wings added to either side, it remained a solid, sturdy structure that suited its surroundings.

She followed the drive to the back of the house, where several other vehicles were parked. As she stepped from the truck she caught sight of an old woman waddling toward her from the barn. The woman was as wide as she was tall, wearing a soiled apron over a long cotton dress that fell to her ankles. Her face was as wrinkled as aged parchment, and her gray hair had been plaited into two fat braids that bounced on her ample bosom.

"Good morning," Ally called cheerfully. "You must be Agnes Tallfeather."

The woman barely paused. "You'd be...?"

"Ally. Allison Brady. I'm here to see Ace."

"Huh. All the pretty ones are." Agnes started past her.

Ally decided to take that as a compliment. "Could you tell me where he is?"

Agnes took the first step and paused to catch her breath. "I could."

Realizing that this was going to be a word game, Ally decided to play along. "Would you, then?"

Agnes climbed the second step. "Barn."

"Thanks." Ally started away. When she glanced back, the old woman had already let herself into the house, leaving the door to slam behind her.

In the barn she followed the sound of voices.

"...Think I'll take some blood, and have Erin run a few tests."

Ally drew closer and caught sight of a tall, rugged rancher standing inside a stall, removing a syringe from his pocket. Just outside the stall were three other men, resting their arms on the wooden rail. The moment she spotted Ace, the others seemed to fade from view.

At that same moment he turned and saw her. His smile did strange things to her heart.

"Ally." He was beside her in a couple of long-legged strides. "I was afraid you wouldn't come."

"And miss the chance to have my truck engine tuned? Not to mention a free meal." She managed a laugh, even though the touch of his hand on her arm had her nerves jumping. "A girl would have to be out of her mind."

She looked up to find the others staring.

"Ally Brady, I'd like you to meet my brother Chance."

She found herself looking up into smiling dark eyes, so like Ace's it was eerie.

"The vampire over there drawing blood is my brother Hazard."

"Hi, Ally." Hazard touched a hand to his wide-brimmed hat, then went back to his work.

"And this is Cody Bridger."

Cody whipped his hat from his head in a courtly gesture. "Ma'am."

"Hello. What am I interrupting?"

"Sick cow. That's Hazard's department. He's the veterinarian. His wife, Erin, is a laboratory researcher and his fellow vampire," Ace said with a laugh. "The two of them get their jollies looking at disgusting things under microscopes."

"Careful." Hazard withdrew the syringe from the animal's rump and pocketed the vial of blood. "We may put you under there next, bro."

Laughing, Ace turned to Cody. "I told Ally to drive her truck over here today. I was hoping, if you don't have too many chores, you'd take at look at the engine.''

''I'd be happy to.''

''Great. How about now?''

''Fine. I'll just fetch my tools.'' The old man started out of the barn.

Ace caught Ally's hand and the two of them followed.

When they were out of earshot, Hazard turned to Chance. ''Where do you suppose he found her?''

Chance grinned. ''You know our little brother. Always the lady-killer. But this one's a knockout. I'll lay odds he didn't find her at a dive like Clancy's.''

Hazard shook his head. ''I'm with you, bro. This one looks like she just dropped down from heaven. Our little brother's taste has certainly improved with age.''

Cody turned to Ace. The two of them had been working under the hood of Ally's truck for more than an hour, while she stood to one side watching. ''There's a small wrench in the toolbox in the barn. Got a broken handle covered with tape. Think you can find it?''

''Sure.'' Ace squeezed Ally's hand, then sauntered off.

''Guess I'll try this again.'' Cody wiped his hands on a rag, then climbed to the cab of the dusty old truck and turned the key in the ignition. The engine caught and purred.

''Ace told me you're a miracle worker, Cody.'' Ally stepped up beside him as he bounded out and ducked his head under the hood one last time.

He turned his head sideways to glance at her. ''This

old truck's in pretty good shape for its age. Must be what…seventy-eight or seventy-nine model?''

''Gramps bought it in seventy-eight. I was five years old, and he said I was the first and only one allowed to ride. Even when I was covered in mud, he'd let me climb up on his lap and pretend to drive it.''

''Sounds like you two had a pretty special relationship.''

She nodded. ''We did. Still do. You ought to meet my grandfather. He's just the best.''

Cody took his time fiddling with a hose, before straightening. ''Met him a time or two.''

''My grandfather? You know him?''

He grinned. ''Don't know him, exactly. Just enough to be thrown off his property.''

''Why?''

'''Cause I worked for the Wildes.'' He looked up, his eyes pinning her. ''Surprised he'd let you drive over here.''

He saw the flush on her cheeks. ''Sorry, ma'am. I see he doesn't know.''

She shook her head. ''Why does he…hate the Wildes, Cody?''

''Don't know. I'm not sure he does either. Wes Wilde was young and brash.'' Cody grinned. ''Ace reminds me a lot of his father.'' He took his time cleaning the grease from his hands. ''Wes wanted to buy Harlan's land. Nothing personal. Just figured he'd own everything between here and the Montana border. Made him a fair enough offer. Harlan refused. Things were said. Feathers ruffled. And two hardheaded men decided never to speak to each other again. It happens that way. And sometimes, unless somebody comes along to question why, it just goes on forever.''

"I..." She stared down at the ground. "I don't want to hurt him."

The old man shrugged. "Truth hurts sometimes. But not telling it can hurt more." He watched her eyes. "You could always just stop seeing Ace. That'd solve everybody's problem."

When she didn't say anything he sighed and muttered, "I think the world of that boy. Wouldn't want to see him conned twice."

"What I did at Clancy's..." She bit her lip. "I'm not proud of it. But I had my reasons."

"Like I said. You could always save everybody's hide if you'd just stop seeing him."

"I wish I could." She shook her head. "I think it's too late for that. For both of us."

He watched her a moment longer, and she thought she saw a flicker of humor behind those eyes. Humor or satisfaction. Then he closed the hood and turned off the engine before touching a hand to the brim of his hat. "Better see to my other chores now, ma'am."

Ace walked up looking proud of himself. "I had to go through every tool in that box, but I found that wrench you wanted, Cody."

The old man took it from him and grinned. "Found out I didn't need it after all." He walked away, leaving Ace to stare after him with a look of puzzlement.

Behind him, Ally watched in stunned silence. It would seem that that old cowboy was quite a con artist himself. He'd just forced her to admit something she hadn't even wanted to admit to herself yet. That she was, against all rhyme or reason, falling helplessly in love with Ace Wilde.

"Hey, Maggie." Ace led Ally into the kitchen, where his sister-in-law was lifting a tray of steaming biscuits from the oven. "I'd like you to meet Ally Brady."

"Hi, Ally. Nice to meet you." Maggie set the tray on a trivet, then removed her oven mitt to shake hands.

Ace broke off a piece of biscuit and popped it into his mouth. "I was hoping to invite Ally to stay for supper."

"Sure. That'd be fine." Maggie picked up a wooden spoon and rapped his knuckles when he went after seconds. "I'm fixing a tenderloin, with a special marinade. And an asparagus salad with artichokes and capers."

Ace kissed her cheek. "I love it when you talk like that."

She grinned. "Get out of here. I know you're just softening me up so you can have another biscuit."

"Did it work?"

She laughed out loud. "Go ahead. Take one. And then get."

Ace snatched up the biscuit and caught Ally's hand. "Come on. I'll give you the grand tour."

In the great room she craned her neck to stare at the massive fireplace that dominated the middle of the room. Around all four sides were sofas drawn up for warmth and conversation.

"It's so big. I think you could put fifty people in here, and not even be crowded."

"Over a hundred," Ace said matter-of-factly. "Both my brothers got married here, and the whole town of Prosperous couldn't fill it." He caught her hand. "Come on. I'll show you Erin's lab."

They walked down a hallway and Ace paused to knock on a door.

A moment later it was opened by a slender young woman who peered from behind round glasses.

"Hey, Erin. I'd like you to meet Ally Brady."

Erin blinked at the beautiful redhead, then offered her hand. "Hi, Ally. Would you like to come inside?"

"Only for a minute," Ally said hesitantly. "I know you must be busy. Ace said you do research."

"For the university. Right now I'm just running a few tests on some blood samples my husband gave me."

She stepped aside and allowed Ally and Ace to precede her into the room. Hazard was seated on a stool, peering through a microscope. He looked up and smiled.

Ally stared around in openmouthed surprise at the well-equipped laboratory. "This looks like something you'd find in a government research facility."

"That's what I thought the first time I saw it." Erin laughed. "The Wildes just like to do everything on a grand scale."

"That's why I married you." Hazard walked up and dropped an arm around his wife's shoulders, pressing a kiss to her temple. "You were the grandest female I'd ever met."

"Oh, you." Erin blushed, and Ally couldn't help laughing.

"Don't mind them. They're newlyweds. Practically still on their honeymoon. And pretty sickening to have to be around." Ace caught her hand. "Come on. I've saved the best for last."

"What's that?" she asked.

He arched a villainous brow. "My room."

"Will I see you later?" Erin called to her retreating back.

"Don't worry," Ace answered for her. "I'm forcing her to stay for some of Maggie's horrible cooking."

"Oh, this is just amazing." Ally took a final bite of tenderloin that melted in her mouth. She had expected to be overwhelmed by Ace's family. Instead she found them to be as easy and relaxed with her as though they'd known her all their lives. She'd toured the house, the barns and the land. Everywhere she went, the people were open and friendly. She'd expected the Wilde operations to be big and impersonal. Instead, they'd proven to be just one big family. "I don't believe I've ever tasted a meal this fine."

"Thank you." Maggie couldn't hide her pleasure at discovering a new admirer. "I'm afraid this whole motley crew is beginning to take me for granted."

"Never." Chance caught his wife's hand and brought it to his lips. "In fact, I've been thinking that it's almost time for another trip to New York, just so you can eat in more fancy restaurants and collect even more fancy recipes. And I can have you all to myself."

"Oh, Chance." She turned to him with shining eyes. "Could we?"

"Absolutely. How about next week?"

She glanced at the others. "See why I love him so?"

Erin couldn't help laughing. "I love Hazard every bit as much as you love Chance. But the thought of flying up to New York every couple of weeks just doesn't appeal to me in the least."

"That's because Hazard has you brainwashed into believing that this whole place will fall apart if he leaves it for even one day."

Ace lifted his glass of wine in a salute. "A smart man, my brother."

Maggie retrieved a tray of fruit tarts, topped with dollops of whipped cream. As they were being passed around the table, she filled their cups with fresh-ground coffee that smelled and tasted like heaven.

"I understand Ace drove you all over the place today, showing you the herds, the range shacks, the wranglers." Erin dipped a fork into her dessert. "What do you think of the Double W, Ally?"

"Amazing. It's so big. I had no idea of the size before today. How did you ever acquire so much land?"

"You don't know the story?" Ace turned to her in surprise.

She shook her head.

He looked across the table. "We've told Ally so many stories today, her head is probably spinning. Why don't you tell her this one, Cody?"

The old cowboy smiled, relishing the idea of repeating the story that had gradually become a legend. "It was back in the early sixties. Nineteen sixty-two. Wes Wilde and his buddy, Mason Gabriel, were a couple of young hustlers working in Vegas. They pooled their money and took on an oil baron, a tobacco heir and a shipping tycoon in a seventy-two-hour poker marathon in Monte Carlo, and wound up with the deed to one hundred fifty thousand acres of prime Wyoming land." He sipped his coffee, clearly enjoying the telling of the tale. "Wes and Mason had never been to Wyoming, so they had no idea just what they'd won. But the minute Wes saw this place, he fell in love. He knew this was where he wanted to be for the rest of his life. Mason, on the other hand, was a city boy, who wanted to sell the land and get back to the business of gambling. Wes tried to talk him into staying, and working the land with him. But Mason refused, so Wes was forced to mortgage everything to buy him out. I heard that within an hour of receiving his money, Mason was on the first plane back to Vegas, where he lived like a big spender.'' He shook his head. ''Poor Wes begged, borrowed and worked himself to death. When he started he didn't know the first thing about ranching. But he learned. And in the end, he was able to pay off the mortgage and have this grand legacy to leave to his sons.''

Ally was clearly moved by the story. She touched a hand to Ace's sleeve. ''I hope your dad lived long enough to see your success.''

He shook his head. ''He died too soon. But I like to think he's watching us.''

''You bet he is, son.'' Cody drained his cup and shoved away from the table. ''Thanks, Maggie. That was a fine dinner, as always. But I got an important card game waiting for me in the bunkhouse.'' He turned to Ally with a smile. ''Good night, ma'am. I hope I'll see you again.''

''Good night, Cody. And thanks again. For fixing my truck. And…everything.''

''Yes'm.'' He crossed the room and plucked his hat from a peg, then stepped out into the night.

''So.'' Chance leaned back. ''Ally, where did you and Ace meet?''

It was the question she'd been dreading all day. She looked at Ace, and realized he wasn't going to help her out. ''We met at Clancy's.''

Hazard nearly choked on his coffee. He exchanged a glance with his older brother. ''At Clancy's?''

''Yeah. I…sort of beat him at a game of eight ball.''

''You beat Ace?'' Chance looked astounded. Then,

as the truth dawned, he threw back his head and roared. "You're the one? The one who hustled him out of a thousand dollars?"

Ally's cheeks were as red as her hair.

"Oh, man, this is just too good." Chance and Hazard howled with laughter. "You should have seen his face the next morning. He was so hot, I'm surprised there weren't rockets going off all over Wyoming."

"Knock it off, Chance." Ace's eyes darkened with anger.

"Do you realize you were the first one who's ever beat him at his own game?"

"I said cut it out." Ace leaned over the table and punched his brother's arm.

"No way. I bet you never told her just how insulted you were. Not because you lost. But because you fell for her con."

"I said that's enough." Ace rounded the table and hauled Chance to his feet by the front of his shirt. But before Ace could land his punch, Chance ducked and Ace's fist smashed into Hazard's shoulder.

"Oh, you just picked on the wrong guy, bro." Hazard countered with a punch of his own, sending Ace flying backward into the kitchen counter.

Maggie calmly removed a tray in danger of being upended, then returned to the table and continued drinking her coffee.

Ally, eyes wide, leapt to her feet. "Isn't anyone going to stop this?"

"Calm down, honey." Erin put a hand on her arm and drew her back to her seat. "They do this all the time. They call it letting off steam. Maggie and I call it brotherly affection."

"Affection..." Ally watched as Ace landed a fist in

his brother's nose, sending blood streaming down the front of Chance's shirt. Chance in turn managed a blow to Ace's chest, sending him stumbling backward, where he stood wheezing in a breath.

"They're going to kill each other," Ally cried.

"Uh-uh. It never goes that far. Though once or twice they've come close." Maggie filled Ally's cup. "Now drink your coffee and ignore them."

"Ignore..." She winced as a fist landed in Hazard's midsection and he went down on one knee. But he managed to get to his feet and retaliate with a blow to Ace's temple that had him reeling.

Ace shook his head to clear his vision. "Had enough?"

Chance was leaning weakly against the kitchen counter. Hazard was steadying himself with a hand on the back of a chair. The two of them looked at each other, then at their brother. Their faces creased into matching grins.

"What?" Ace demanded. "What's so funny?"

"You," Chance said. "In this crazy world, it seems perfectly natural that you'd fall for the only woman who could ever beat you at your own game."

Ally waited for another fight. Instead, she was amazed to see Ace's lips turning in a smile. "Yeah. It's crazy, all right. But there it is."

The three brothers fell together, arms around each other, laughing hysterically.

"See?" Maggie turned to Ally. "It happens every time. You may as well get used to it."

Ally shook her head. "I don't think so. I don't think I could ever get used to such a spectacle."

"You will." Maggie smiled across the table at Erin. "Actually, I'd discovered that it really does seem to

The Silhouette Reader Service™ —Here's how it works:

Accepting your 2 free books and gift places you under no obligation to buy anything. You may keep the books and gift and return the shipping statement marked "cancel." If you do not cancel, about a month later we'll send you 6 additional novels and bill you just $3.80 each in the U.S., or $4.21 each in Canada, plus 25¢ delivery per book and applicable taxes if any.* That's the complete price and — compared to cover prices of $4.50 each in the U.S. and $5.25 each in Canada — it's quite a bargain! You may cancel at any time, but if you choose to continue, every month we'll send you 6 more books, which you may either purchase at the discount price or return to us and cancel your subscription.

*Terms and prices subject to change without notice. Sales tax applicable in N.Y. Canadian residents will be charged applicable provincial taxes and GST.

If offer card is missing write to: Silhouette Reader Service, 3010 Walden Ave., P.O. Box 1867, Buffalo, NY 14240-1867

BUSINESS REPLY MAIL
FIRST-CLASS MAIL   PERMIT NO. 717   BUFFALO, NY

POSTAGE WILL BE PAID BY ADDRESSEE

SILHOUETTE READER SERVICE
3010 WALDEN AVE
PO BOX 1867
BUFFALO NY 14240-9952

NO POSTAGE
NECESSARY
IF MAILED
IN THE
UNITED STATES

clear the air. Though I don't recommend it for anyone except those three clowns.''

As Maggie began gathering up the dishes, Ally started to help her.

"Sorry." Chance turned from the sink, where he'd washed away the blood, and took the dishes from her hands. "I can't let you do my job.''

"You do the dishes?''

He shot her a grin, and she was reminded of Ace's heart-stopping smile. Apparently it ran in the family. They were all handsome, charming and certifiably crazy. "I like being alone with my wife. So the rest of you had better find someplace to go. Fast.''

Hazard caught Erin's hand. "Come on. I think I've just thought of the perfect way to spend a Saturday night.''

"In the lab?''

"Some place even better.''

She blushed and turned to Ally. "I'm so glad we met. I do hope Ace brings you here again.''

"Thanks." Ally turned to Maggie. "And thanks again for the wonderful dinner. But, since you won't let me help you clean up, I think I'd better head on home.''

"So soon?" Ace caught her hand.

"Yeah. I've left Gramps alone all day. Besides...'' She looked him up and down. "You've got to change your clothes. Those are bloodstained.''

"All the more reason to stay. You could help me change.''

"Yeah. In your dreams.''

Ace followed her out the door to her truck. Before she could open the door he leaned close and covered her lips with his. "I wish you wouldn't run off. You heard my brother. It's Saturday night. Why don't we sneak up to my room and…find something to do?''

Despite the jolt to her system, she managed to laugh. ''If I were a teacher I'd give you an A for effort. But I'd have to give you a failing grade for that line.''

''Pretty lame, huh?''

''Yeah. As bad as all the others you've tried.''

''Then how about this one?'' He crushed her against him and kissed her long and slow and deep, until she felt her bones melting and her blood pounding in her temples.

''Oh, Ace. You make it awfully hard to refuse.'' She reached a hand to his cheek and brushed her lips over his.

At once she absorbed the jolt and took a step backward. She saw his eyes narrow, but to his credit, he made no move to touch her again. They both knew that if he did, neither of them would be able to stop.

Without taking time to think it through she said, ''I owe you. For my truck, and the lovely dinner. And that…fascinating fight scene.''

''So how are you going to pay up?''

''By inviting you to dinner tomorrow night.''

His smile was dazzling. ''It's a date.''

She climbed up into the truck and turned the key. The engine purred. ''I can't get over how much better it's running. That is just the sweetest thing.''

''No. This is.'' He leaned inside the open window and kissed her, hard and quick.

She felt the nervous jitter along her spine, and then the surge of heat through her veins. He had the most devastating effect on her system.

''Now get out of here fast, before I carry you off to my room and have my way with you.''

As she put the truck in gear and started away, she studied him in the rearview mirror. So tall and handsome and rugged. Funny and sweet and charming. She'd watched him with his family. They were as devoted to him as he was to them. He was, she realized, everything she'd ever wanted.

Chapter 8

With a smile of satisfaction Ally surveyed the kitchen. She'd taken such pains with everything. She wanted tonight to be perfect. She'd walked the fields early that morning, picking an armload of Indian paintbrush. Their bright orange blooms were in vases everywhere. On the counters and windowsills, and a low round vase of them sat in the middle of the table. She'd added some yellow roses that she'd found blooming on a broken trellis by the side of the barn. She remembered seeing those same roses when she was a little girl. It had been such a delight to find them still surviving after all these years.

Like her and Gramps, she thought. Still here.

The table was set with brightly colored place mats. The steaks were marinating on a platter beside the oven. Next to them was a tray of steaming biscuits. Ally broke one open to assure herself that they were perfect. She'd already tossed away her first two attempts, when she'd left them in the oven too long, and they'd come out too crisp.

She had resisted the idea of baking potatoes. Too ordinary. Instead she'd opted for an exotic recipe calling for sliced potatoes, onion and grated cheese. For dessert she'd baked a lavish flan. A sponge cake which she'd very carefully divided into layers and slathered with whipped cream. On top she'd arranged perfect circles of fruit. Sliced strawberries. Kiwi. Plump blueberries. Perfect raspberries. All in lovely symmetry. It looked almost too pretty to eat.

Not as fancy as Maggie's dinner of the previous night, but a meal a man could enjoy.

After a glance at the clock she hurried upstairs to change. She'd planned the perfect outfit. Different from anything Ace had ever seen her in before. Unlike the jeans she'd been wearing that first night. Or the uptight business clothes she wore to work. This was a simple sundress of cool mint-green silk, with cap sleeves that fluttered at her upper arms, and a softly scalloped sweetheart neckline. The fabric molded itself to her curves and fell in a straight column to her ankles. On her feet were little strappy sandals.

She brushed her hair long and loose, then decided to be flirtateous by scooping up one side behind her ear with a jeweled comb. The effect was deadly.

She couldn't help laughing as she moved around her room, lighting scented candles. That done, she added more candles in the bathroom.

Ace Wilde didn't have a chance.

She was giggling as she made her way downstairs. Nerves, she realized. She'd never before planned a seduction. But she'd spent most of the night tossing and turning, until she'd realized that this was what she wanted. Ace was what she wanted.

It wasn't really a seduction, she consoled herself. After all, Ace had made it plain that this was what he wanted, too. She was just going to make it easy for him.

She headed out to the barn.

"Gramps?"

At the sight of her Buster and Billy leapt to their feet and hurried over to rub their noses into her hands. She complied by petting them and scratching behind their ears until they were wiggling with delight.

Harlan looked up from his work table. "Why, Allycat. Don't you look pretty."

"Thanks." She smiled and walked up to press a kiss to his cheek. "I've come to bring you inside to clean up."

"Clean up? What for?"

"For dinner." She gave a shake of her head. "You've forgotten."

"Oh." He looked sheepish. "Sorry. I guess I did. Got too engrossed in this project." He showed her the beginnings of a saddle he was working on. "Can't you and Ace have dinner alone?"

"We could. But I'd like you there, Gramps." She had decided that she would tell him the truth about Ace. And then, with the air cleared of any misunderstanding, she would be free to reveal her true feelings for the son of his old enemy. His old *ex*-enemy, she reminded herself.

"Okay. Tell you what. I'll come up to the house when Ace gets here. Until then, I'd like to keep working on this."

"He ought to be here any minute."

He saw the little frown that wrinkled her brow. "Don't worry. I'll hear his truck."

She gave a sigh of exasperation and turned away. "All right."

As she started out the two dogs followed, running ahead when they realized she was going back to the house. Inside she rewarded them with a dish of water, then decided to go upstairs and check her appearance.

She added gloss to her lips, and dabbed perfume at her throat. Hearing the sound of Ace's truck, she raced down the stairs and hurried out on the porch to greet him.

In her haste the door slammed and she was aware that she'd left the dogs inside. No matter. They barked for only a minute, then fell silent. Apparently they'd come to accept Ace as one of the family, too.

He stepped out of the truck and bounded toward her, carrying a bouquet of flowers. The moment he spotted her he stopped dead in his tracks.

"Wow." It was all he could manage.

"I hope that means you approve?"

"You look…" He shook his head. "Red, you're so beautiful, it scares me."

Her heart nearly burst with joy. "Good. I like a little fear in a man." She glanced at the flowers. "Are those for me? Or are you saving them for Gramps?"

He grinned and her heart did another series of flips. "For you." He held them out. "But they look awfully plain next to what I'm looking at."

She opened the tissue wrappings and gaped at the mass of white roses. Then, because she was afraid she'd embarrass herself by weeping, she buried her face in them and breathed them in. "Oh, Ace, they're wonderful."

Cradling them to her chest she took his arm. "Come on. We'll have to drag Gramps away from his workroom. I've already called him once, but he insisted on working until you got here. By now he's probably so immersed in his work, he'll have forgotten about everything else."

At the door to the barn she called, "Gramps, Ace is here."

Harlan looked up, peering over his shoulder. "Well. Ace. I didn't hear your truck."

Ally turned to Ace with a smile. "I told you." To her grandfather she said, "Are you ready for dinner?"

He set down his tools and pressed a button on the scooter, turning it away from the workbench. "It looks like I'd better be."

As Ace and Ally walked ahead of him, he trailed along until they came to the porch. While they climbed the steps, he rolled up the ramp. Ace opened the door and waited for Ally and Harlan to precede him.

"I'll have to find a vase for these." Ally turned to Ace. "And maybe you can open the bottle of champagne."

"Champagne?" Ace's smile widened. "This sounds like a serious occasion."

She blushed. "I just thought…" She shrugged and led the way into the kitchen, with the men trailing behind her. "…After that lovely dinner at your place last night, I'd…"

The words died in her throat. At the sight that greeted her, she froze.

Puzzled, Ace and Harlan moved around her, to see what had rendered her speechless.

There was broken glass littering every inch of the kitchen floor. In the middle of it all lay Buster and

Billy, busily devouring the last of the steaks. The rolls were scattered everywhere. One was even stuck to Buster's paw.

For a moment everyone simply stared at the chaos in silence. Then, as the ridiculousness of the situation struck them, Ace and Harlan burst into gales of laughter.

Laughter? Ally turned on them with a killing look. "How can you laugh? This isn't funny."

"Not funny? Allycat." Harlan was shaking with laughter. "Look at those two old critters. Look at their faces. Have you ever seen two more satisfied dogs in your life?"

"Dogs?" Her voice lowered with a fury that nearly choked her. "They're not dogs. They're pigs. Both of them." She ran at them, waving her bouquet of roses like a wild woman, scattering leaves and petals everywhere. "Get out of here. Shoo, you disgusting creatures. Go on. Get."

Alarmed, Billy started yapping and leapt on his hind feet, dancing in circles.

This only had Ace and Harlan laughing harder.

Buster lifted his head to burp loudly. Then he managed to finish the last bite of steak before getting slowly to his feet. As he backed away from Ally, he left the remains of a broken crystal plate and shattered flan cake that had been smashed beneath his rump.

"No. Oh, no. Not my flan, too." Ally stopped and stared at the mass of crumbs and whipped cream and scattered fruit, then picked up a dish towel and started waving it at the two dogs.

"Out. Get out of here."

While the two men could do nothing but howl with laugher, Ally chased the two dogs through the house.

Minutes later the door slammed, and her footsteps could be heard returning.

When she entered the kitchen her eyes were little points of flame. Two bright spots of color rode high on her cheeks. She turned her anger on the two men who were nearly doubled over.

"You think it's funny, do you?" She knew her voice was trembling, but she couldn't help herself. She knew, too, that she was close to tears. To keep from crying, she focused on her anger. "Who's going to clean this mess? And what am I supposed to fix for dinner now? Now that those two…pigs have eaten everything I've slaved over."

"Look. Settle down now." Ace was trying to contain his laughter. But the more he tried, the more it bubbled up, until he had to wipe tears from his eyes. "Come here, Red."

He led her across the room, picking his way through the food and shards of glass, until he pushed her down onto one of the kitchen chairs. "Just sit here. I'll open the champagne."

"Why? What's to celebrate?"

"We'll think of something." Minutes later, after a loud pop, Ace filled three flutes and handed one to Harlan before carrying the other two across the room. As he handed her the glass he said, "Here's to…" He choked back his laughter. "…A memorable evening."

That had her chin coming up and her eyes narrowing.

"Don't move." He took a sip of champagne, then turned to Harlan. "Where's a broom and dustpan?"

"In there." Harlan pointed to the laundry room.

Ace returned and began to sweep, casting glances at Harlan as he did. He moved through the debris, picking up broken roses and bundling them into a lopsided, sad-looking bouquet, which he set in the sink.

The two men were like naughty children in church. The more they tried to hold back the laughter, the more impossible it became, until they were simply out of control. With each step Ace took, he laughed harder. After dumping the last of the mess in a wastebasket, he crumpled onto a chair and laughed until he was struggling for breath. "Did Billy ever perform in a circus?"

Harlan wiped his eyes. "You mean the way he dances around in circles?"

"Yeah." Ace glanced at Ally, but she had turned away to stare out the window.

"Ally taught him that one summer. She used to wave a treat over his head and make him dance before she'd give it to him."

"No wonder he was dancing. Those were some treats they had today."

The two men convulsed with laughter again.

When he could find his voice Ace looked around. "Well. I've cleaned up the mess." He spotted a roll under one of the cabinets. "Most of it, anyway. Now what'll we fix for dinner?" He glanced at Ally. "Is there anything left that Buster and Billy haven't ruined?"

She shrugged. Sniffed the air. And let out a shriek. "Oh, no. My potatoes."

She rushed across the room and yanked open the oven door. Smoke billowed out. Grabbing a pair of oven mitts she hauled the burned mess over to the sink and turned on the taps. At once a spray of steam rolled around the room.

Ace opened the door and windows and Harlan propelled his scooter out to the patio.

When Ally stepped out and sank down on a patio chair she said, "The only thing left of my dinner is some ice cream. Lucky for us Buster and Billy couldn't open the freezer. And I couldn't burn it to a crisp."

Ace swallowed hard. This wasn't the time to let her see the laughter that still threatened. "Okay. That's a start. Now for an entrée. How about..." He thought a moment. "Hamburgers on the grill?"

"Suits me," Harlan called.

Ally shook her head. "There's ground beef in the freezer. But it'll be solid as a brick."

"Okay." He thought again. "How about grilled cheese sandwiches?"

"There's bread and cheese in the fridge," Harlan said.

Ace went back to the kitchen to search for the bread and cheese. Ally followed and located a skillet.

"This is silly. I invited you to eat, not to fix dinner."

"Nope." Ace took the skillet from her hand. "You sip your champagne. I'll take care of this."

He lit the flame beneath the pan, then a few minutes later began flipping sandwiches until they were golden brown, and the cheese was dripping out the sides.

"Just the way I like them," Harlan remarked as he took the first bite of his.

"Me, too." Ace grinned. "How's yours, Red?"

"Fine." She chewed woodenly. Swallowed. "Just fine."

"Nothing like a perfect grilled cheese, washed down with cool champagne." Ace winked at her, and lifted his glass in a toast, and she knew she couldn't stay angry forever. Her lips twitched. Against her will she laughed.

"There now." Ace closed a hand over hers. "There's that smile. I knew I'd see it before very long."

Harlan polished off his sandwich and looked up. "How about that ice cream, Allycat?"

"Oh, yeah." She went inside and filled three dishes, then located some fudge sauce which she heated and poured over each.

"Now this was worth waiting for." Harlan dug in.

"Gramps." Ally took in a breath. Even though the first part of her plan had gone awry, there was no reason why she couldn't follow through on the rest. As long as he was feeling mellow, the time was right. "There's something I want to tell…" Out of the corner of her eye she saw two furry creatures slinking around the corner of the house. "Buster. Billy."

At the sound of her voice they came rushing up, tongues licking, bodies wriggling.

"Oh, no you don't." She glowered at them. "You're not worming your way back into my good graces that easily. Now, go lie down."

"You know you're going to forgive them," Harlan said with a laugh.

"Yeah. Eventually. Oh, what the heck." She reached out to scratch behind their ears.

Just then Buster put his head in her lap and looked up at her with those big soulful eyes. It was enough to melt even the hardest of hearts.

"Looks like he's telling you he's sorry," Harlan said with a laugh.

"Yeah." She sighed. "I guess I'll have to…" Before she could finish, the old dog gagged. And deposited his entire meal down the front of her dress.

She fled to her room in tears.

Ally pinned her hair on top of her head and stepped into the shower. Minutes later she emerged and rummaged through her drawers for something to wear. She finally settled on an old pair of denim shorts and a simple little summer blouse that tied at her midriff.

She scowled at her reflection in the mirror. Not exactly the effect she'd wanted. But it no longer mattered. The whole evening had gone downhill.

Barefoot she walked around the room snuffing the candles, then did the same in the bathroom. There was no need for pretty scents and soft flickering light. No need to set the mood for something that wasn't to be.

When she walked downstairs she found Ace cleaning the last of the dishes. The roses, which had seemed so stunning when he'd first presented them to her, now looked tired and wilted in their vase. The room still reeked of burned potatoes.

She glanced around. "Where's Gramps?"

"He went off to his workroom. He took the chow hounds with him."

"But I wanted to talk to him."

"He said he'd see you in the morning."

She frowned. "Well, why not? Everything else has gone wrong tonight. I don't see why I expected anything to be salvaged out of this mess."

"Hey. Stop beating yourself up." He placed his hands on her shoulders and stared down into her eyes. "I know this wasn't what you'd planned. But I have to admit, I had a great time. I don't know when I've laughed this hard."

"Yeah. We're a laugh a minute." She pushed aside the feelings that shivered through her at his touch. "I think—" she turned away, so she wouldn't have to see his face "—we ought to call it a night. You have a long drive ahead of you. And we both have to work in the morning."

His voice lowered with feeling. "If you'd say the word, I could be spared that long drive."

She could feel him playing with her hair. It sent little tremors of fire and ice curling along her spine.

She shook her head. "Sorry. The timing's just wrong."

"Timing?" There was a thread of anger in his tone. "Red, our timing's been wrong since our very first meeting. And that hasn't stopped us so far."

She drew her arms around herself, refusing to look at him. "I don't want to argue with you, Ace. I just want you to go."

There was silence for the longest time, and she knew he was staring at her, trying to gauge the depth of her anger.

"Okay." He spoke the word on a sigh of resignation.

Without another word he brushed past her and made his way to the front door. She heard the door open and close, and heard the sound of his footsteps crunching on gravel as he made his way to his truck.

In the silence that followed she heard the sound of the truck door being opened and slammed shut. Heard the sound of the engine as he turned the key in the ignition.

She wasn't even aware that she was running through the house. Out the door. Along the path. Though her feet were bare, she took no notice of the bits of stone

and gravel that cut and scraped her tender flesh. All
she could think of was the fact that she couldn't let
him go. Not like this.

"Ace."

Her voice drifted through the open window of the
truck. His foot hit the brake pedal, and he brought the
truck to a halt.

"What did I forget?" He threw the gear into park
and waited.

"Nothing. This isn't about you. It's about me. About
what I forgot."

"And that is?"

"An apology."

"What do you have to apologize for?"

"My temper. I'm not mad at you. I'm not even mad
at the silly dogs. I'm really mad at myself. You see, I
wanted everything to be perfect tonight because…"
She took a deep breath and forced herself to say the
words before she lost her nerve. "I intended to seduce
you after dinner."

"You…" He was so thunderstruck, he couldn't
think of a thing to say. Very deliberately he turned off
the engine and opened the truck door, pocketing the
key as he did. Then he leaned against the door of the
truck and crossed his arms over his chest. "You were
going to seduce me?"

She nodded.

"How?"

"Well, I was…" Flustered, she struggled to think.
"Well, by setting the perfect scene. That dress. My
hair. I saw how you looked at me when you first saw
me."

"Red, the dress and hair were perfect. But they
weren't what I was seeing."

"They weren't?"

He shook his head. "I was seeing you. The same way I'm seeing you now. So, I'll ask you again. How were you planning to go about seducing me?"

She shrugged, feeling suddenly awkward and shy. "I figured we'd start by kissing."

He stood very still. "Care to show me?"

She stepped closer and brushed her lips over his. The flare of heat was instantaneous. She felt it from the top of her head all the way to her toes.

Disappointment washed over her when he didn't kiss her back. In fact, except for a slight narrowing of his eyes, he didn't react at all. He simply stood there, watching her in the shimmer of moonlight.

"I guess...I guess that wasn't very good. I don't have much experience in seduction."

Over his dry throat he managed to ask, "Did you have anything else planned?"

"I thought I'd..." Instead of telling him, she decided to show him. She lifted a hand to the pins in her hair. As soon as they were removed it tumbled in fiery waves around her shoulders. She saw his hands drop to his sides, where they clenched into fists.

"And then I'd..." She reached a hand to the buttons of her blouse and saw the way he watched her.

Something dangerous flared in his eyes as she unbuttoned first one, and then another. He waited to see her slide the blouse from her shoulders. Instead, he was disappointed when she gathered the edges together in one hand and suddenly hung her head.

"I guess I was feeling a lot bolder when I was imagining all this. I didn't realize one of us would be doing all the work, and the other would be just watching from the sidelines."

"Oh. You want my participation, do you?"

She nodded. "That would be nice."

"Nice?" His lips curved in a dangerous smile. "Careful, Red. Nice isn't in my vocabulary. If I join in this little game, it won't be any half measure. If I'm in, I'm in all the way. And we won't stop until I say so."

At his words, spoken so softly, her heart leapt to her throat. "You make it sound like a...war."

"That's what it'll feel like. Mortal combat. No-holds-barred. Like a knock-down-drag-out pool hustle. Only for much higher stakes." He shot her a challenging look. "Are you in?"

He still hadn't moved. And yet she could almost feel his hands on her. Could already feel the heat beginning to flow through her veins like molten lava. "You mean, you'd still be interested? After all that went wrong?"

"I'm asking you, Red. Are you in?"

She swallowed. Nodded.

Before she could say a word his hand snaked out, catching her by the wrist and dragging her into his arms. And then his mouth, that warm, clever mouth, was on hers. And those strong fingers were moving over her as he took her on a wild, dizzying ride.

He lifted his head and she filled her lungs with deep draughts of warm night air.

"Either we continue this inside, Red—" he pressed his lips to a tangle of hair at her temple "—or I'm going to end up taking you right here in the dirt."

She glanced up. "You wouldn't."

"Wouldn't I?" He chuckled, a deep rich sound that trickled over her nerves like warm honey. "You're talking to a starving man, Red. One who's standing before a banquet. And I can't wait to eat my fill.'' He nibbled her cheek, her ear. ''Your call.''

Despite the weakness that held her in its grip, she caught his hand and began sprinting toward the house, with him in tow.

Chapter 9

They made it as far as the porch. With a laugh she opened the door and led him inside. But then she made a tactical error. She turned to him, intending to lead him up the stairs.

At the mere touch of her hand he made an animal sound low in his throat and dragged her against him, savaging her mouth with a hunger that left her gasping.

"Ace. Wait." She pushed against him.

"Too late." He kissed her again and thrilled to her moan of pleasure.

When she surfaced she managed a laugh. "I only meant we could go upstairs."

"We'll never make it." He was already sliding her shirt from her shoulders and tearing aside the bit of lace that covered her breasts. And then he was feasting and she was helpless to do more than give herself up to the feelings. Feelings that had her whimpering with a pleasure that bordered on pain.

"You're so beautiful. So perfect." His words, whispered against her flesh, had her shivering. "All big green eyes and skin like cream." He ran wet nibbling kisses up the column of her throat and buried his lips in the sensitive hollow of her throat. "And I want to devour you until I've had my fill."

"Ace." She brought her hands to his face, hoping to still his movements. "I need a moment. I can't think."

"Don't think." He flashed that quick, dangerous smile. "Just feel."

He caught her hand and placed it to his heart. It was thundering like a herd of mustangs. "Feel what you do to me."

He lowered his head to her. His mouth moved over hers, slowly, deliberately, until her lips parted for him. His tongue tangled with hers, teasing, tempting, until she sighed and wrapped her arms around his neck and kissed him back.

His lips whispered over her face, pressing kisses to her eyelids, her cheeks, the tip of her nose.

"Oh, Red." He breathed her name inside her mouth, and she thought of how she'd once hated that nickname. On his lips it sounded like the most beautiful name in the world.

His tongue traced the curve of her ear, nipping and tugging on the lobe, before darting inside, sending her pulse rate climbing.

When she shivered and tried to pull away he dragged her even closer and burned a trail of hot, wet kisses down her throat. He could feel the wild, erratic rhythm of her pulse-beat. As ragged as his own. And the way her breath hitched in her throat on a near sob.

The spicy fragrance was stronger here at the base of her throat. A perfume that filled his lungs and went straight to his head.

''I need to touch you.'' She tugged his shirt from his waistband and slipped it over his head. And then her hands were on his chest, up his arms, over his shoulders. With each movement, she could feel his muscles tense, his heartbeat accelerate.

He was so strong. The feel of him, all hard muscle and sleek sinew, gave her a thrill. And yet, for all his strength, there was a tenderness in him that was completely unexpected. And so out of character, it never ceased to move her.

He brought his hand to the waistband of her shorts and nearly tore them in his haste. Underneath was another bit of lace that was stripped away with a single tug. At last he was free to see her. All of her. And the sight of her made his throat go dry.

It occurred to him, in one breathless moment, that he could take her here and now. It was what they both wanted. Then they would be free of this terrible tension that was threatening to turn them both into raging animals. But it wouldn't be enough. He wanted more. He wanted it all.

He'd fantasized about this. Had dreamed of all the ways he would love her. And now he was free to do all those wonderful, glorious things he'd only hoped for. And so he banked the need and lowered his face, skimming soft butterfly kisses over her face.

Moonlight streamed through the skylights, turning her hair to flame, her skin to burnished gold. When he brought his mouth lower, to the smooth column of her throat, she arched her neck to give him easier access.

But just as she began to relax, he cupped her breasts in his hands and rubbed his work-roughened thumbs across the peaks.

He saw those lovely green eyes darken. Heard the hiss of breath as she grew more and more aroused. Felt the way her body moved under his, inviting him to take more.

And he did. He found her hot and moist, and drove her to the first frenzied peak. He saw the way her eyes widened, then slowly glazed with passion. For the moment, she was his. Only his.

This was how he'd wanted her. Weak with desire. Oblivious to all except him. He watched the play of emotions on her face as she slowly surfaced.

Giddy with need she reached for the fasteners at his waist. He helped her, shrugging out of his boots, his jeans. His briefs were shredded as they both tugged them aside, laughing like children.

Their clothes lay in tangles around them, beneath them, and Ace and Ally were at last lying flesh to flesh.

His eyes, dark and fierce, were steady on hers as he kissed her long and slow and deep. He heard the purr of pleasure deep in her throat as he ran openmouthed kisses down her neck, over her breasts, then lower. Her body jerked in violent response when he moved lower still. He heard her gasp as another climax ripped through her. He gave her no time to recover as, with lips and teeth and tongue, he took her on a wild ride to places she'd never even dreamed of. Even while her body shuddered, she hungered for more.

And he gave. With a recklessness even he had never known before, he drove her higher, then higher still.

He knew he was gripped by madness. Knew that

there was something building inside that would soon demand to be set free. But he had slipped beyond reason, beyond control. Blinded by hard, driving need, he linked his fingers with hers and stared into her eyes, needing to see her as he entered her.

Her body was slick with sheen. She tangled her arms and legs with his, wrapping herself around him with a strength that surprised him.

And then she was moving with him. Climbing with him.

Lungs straining, hearts racing, they sprinted to the very top of the mountain. And then, as their bodies trembled and shuddered, he cried out her name, or thought he did, as they stepped out into the abyss. And soared.

"It's a good thing this evening didn't go as you'd planned." Still joined, Ace pressed his forehead to hers and dragged in a breath. "If it had, you'd have killed me, Red. Or we'd have killed each other."

She gave a weak sound that might have been a laugh. "You mean we're not dead?"

"I'm not sure. Are you all right?" Ace lifted a hand to brush the hair from her eye.

"Fine." She rubbed a thumb over his mouth. "I'm fine."

"Yeah." His smile was quick and deadly. "Better than fine. You, Red, were definitely worth waiting for."

"And that was," she sighed, "some pool hustle. Got any more moves, cowboy?"

"I've got a million of 'em."

"I'll bet you have."

He closed his eyes. "Do you know how long I've wanted you, Red?"

She smiled. "Since the first time you saw me."

His eyes blinked open. "How would you know that?"

"It's an old line, Ace. Couldn't you have thought of a better one?"

He rolled aside and lay back, his hands under his head, his lips curved into a satisfied smile. "Call it a line if you want. It's the truth. I saw those long, long legs and that great backside draped over a pool table and told myself that this was some kind of woman. I couldn't take my eyes off you, Red."

"I noticed. Of course, I wasn't exactly trying to be invisible. The truth is, I spotted you the minute you walked into Clancy's."

"Then you're one hell of an actress. You never once looked my way. All I could see was you smiling at all those other cowboys. And I hated every one of them."

"Part of my plan. Never let your mark see you watching him. And never let him know you're interested."

"Next you're going to tell me you planned to get nearly run over by that waitress with a tray of drinks."

She laughed, that wonderful rich sound that whispered over his senses.

His eyes widened. "You didn't! You saw it coming?"

"Well, everything except the way you grabbed me. I figured you'd pull me out of her way. But I hadn't been counting on..." She traced a finger along his upper arm. "...All these rock-hard muscles. That caught me by surprise."

"You're full of surprises yourself, Red." He reached out and drew her into the circle of his arms. "Warm enough?"

"Any hotter and I'd think we left the oven on." She suddenly looked alarmed and started to sit up. "We did remember to turn it off, didn't we?"

"Yeah. Relax." He drew her close and pressed his lips to a tangle of hair at her temple. "All the bad luck of this night is behind us."

"You think so?"

"Mmm-hmm. Trust me. We broke the jinx." He sniffed the air. "What's that smell?"

"What smell?"

"Like a funeral parlor. Or a flower shop."

"Oh. That." She snuggled closer, loving the feel of his arms around her. "I had scented candles burning upstairs in the bedroom and bath. Part of my planned seduction."

"You thought of everything, didn't you?" He grinned. "Pretty dangerous, considering your luck tonight. You could have burned the house down."

"I know." She shrugged. "It doesn't matter. I blew them out. Besides." She began playing with the hair on his chest. "My luck did get better."

"Yeah." He could feel the need for her rising again. "So did mine. And if you don't stop that, we both might get lucky right this minute."

"That's impossible. We couldn't again. You're just bragging."

"You ought to know by now that I never brag unless I can back it up." He caught a strand of her hair and watched as it sifted between his fingers. Then he looked into her eyes. "Want to call my bluff?"

She absorbed the quick sexual tug deep inside. Would he always have this effect on her? One look, one touch, and she was lost. "Okay, Superman. You're on. I don't believe you."

He looked at her with that devastating smile that never failed to go straight to her heart. Without warning he dragged her close and kissed her until she was breathless. Against her mouth he whispered, "I'm going to love proving you wrong, Red."

And then, without words, he took her on a long slow journey that had her bones melting and her mind swept clean of all thought except him.

"Ace?" Ally rolled over and was dismayed to find the bed empty.

The sky was still dark outside the bedroom windows. Some time during the night he had carried her up the stairs to her bed. But, though they'd managed a few hours' sleep, most of the night had been spent in lovemaking.

They couldn't seem to get enough of each other. It was as if a dam had burst, and all their feelings were finally free to spill over. At times their loving had burned with all the intensity of a summer storm. At other times they were as easy, as comfortable with each other as if they'd been together for a lifetime.

But now she found herself alone. She touched a hand to his pillow. It still bore the warmth of his head.

"Looking for me?"

He switched on a bedside lamp, filling the room with light, then turned on the ceiling fan overhead.

At her arched brow he explained, "You've been

generating too much heat, Red. And I've exerted so much energy, I needed to replenish it.''

He was barefoot and shirtless, wearing only his jeans, leaving the snaps undone. Over his arm was an array of clothing. ''I found these downstairs and thought I'd haul them along.''

She studied the tray in his hands. ''I'm not interested in the clothes right now. Just show me the food.''

''There's champagne.'' He lifted the half-filled bottle and poured two flutes. ''No sense letting this go flat.'' He handed one to her and sipped the other. Then he climbed into bed and set a napkin-covered plate between them.

Ally sat up, unmindful of her nakedness, and sipped her champagne while staring at the plate. ''What did you fix?''

''My specialty.'' He whipped the napkin off and lifted half a sandwich to her mouth. ''Taste.''

She bit into it, chewed, swallowed. Then looked over at him. ''Peanut butter?''

He grinned. ''It was all I could find. Those cupboards leave something to be desired.''

''Yeah, I haven't really taken time to shop yet. We're not exactly located near convenient shopping centers.''

''Hey. I'm not complaining. The truth is, I love peanut butter sandwiches. They kept me alive for a lot of years.'' He took a bite, then offered it to her.

''How did you and your brothers decide who would do the cooking?''

''The rule was, whoever caved in to hunger first had to cook for all. You can imagine that my brothers and I managed to go hungry a lot, rather than have to do the cooking for each other. But Thelma Banks, the owner of the E.Z. Diner in Prosperous used to send along care packages whenever one of us went to town."

Ally arched a brow. "I remember Thelma. We used to stop by her diner all the time when I was a kid."

"Everybody knows Thelma. She's a fixture in Prosperous. A real character. But she has a heart of gold." He topped off their glasses and plumped up his pillow before leaning back. "And then Agnes Tallfeather decided to adopt us. Her husband Louis used to do odd jobs around the ranch. He and Agnes never had any kids of their own, and I think we filled a void in her life. Anyway, she's probably the world's worst cook. But we didn't care, as long as we didn't have to go near the kitchen."

"Did Agnes raise you?"

He laughed. "We were pretty much raised by the time we lost our dad. Hazard was fifteen and Chance was seventeen." He shook his head. "Looking back, I realize I must have given them plenty of bad moments. Even at twelve, I was pretty wild. There wasn't anything I wouldn't try at least once."

"Such as?"

He offered her half of the remaining half sandwich, then polished off the rest and washed it down with champagne. "I crashed my first airplane when I was still in high school."

"You...crashed? Were you hurt?"

He chuckled, remembering. "Just a lot of cuts and bruises. I remember limping away. But the plane was demolished, and we still had two years to pay for it.

And there was the truck I flipped over in a snow-storm.''

"How old were you when that happened?''

"Thirteen. I figured if I was old enough to drive a tractor, I was old enough to take the truck into town.''

"Oh, Ace, your poor brothers.''

"Yeah." He reached over and linked his fingers with hers. "I'd hate to have a kid like me. He'd give me heart failure.''

"I don't know.'' She glanced at their linked hands, feeling a curl of pleasure along her spine and wonder-ing at the warm tremors his simple touch caused. "Considering the way you've turned out, I'd say you'd be lucky.''

"Know something, Red?" He set aside his glass and drew her close to brush his lips over hers. "Right now, I'm feeling like the luckiest guy in the world." He took her glass from her hands and placed it next to his. Then he slid his hands down her arms and watched her eyes warm and soften. "Now that I'm fortified, why don't I show you a few more of my smooth moves?"

She laughed. "You mean there are a few we've missed?"

"Yeah. There's this." He pulled her down amid the sheets and plunged his hands into her hair, causing her to giggle. "And this." He ran nibbling kisses along the column of her throat, eliciting more laughter. "And this." He brought his mouth lower, nibbling and suck-ling until her laughter turned to a gasp of pleasure.

And then there were no more words as they lost themselves in the wonder of love.

Ally lay perfectly still, loving the feel of Ace's body beside hers. She lay with her back to him, snuggled close against him. His arms were around her, his lips buried against her neck. He had one leg thrown possessively across hers.

The first rays of morning sunlight threaded their way across the sky. A chorus of birds had begun to greet the day.

"You awake?" His voice, rough with sleep, sent shivers of pleasure along her spine.

"Mmm-hmm." It seemed too much effort to speak. She stifled a yawn. "I suppose we should think about getting up."

"Not yet." His hand found her breast and he felt the nipple harden instantly at his touch. He nibbled a trail of kisses across her shoulder, while his other hand began a lazy exploration of her hip and thigh.

She sighed from the pure pleasure of his touch. But as the pressure increased, and her need for him grew, her sighs turned to moans. She tried to turn toward him but his leg pinned her, holding her still.

She was aware of his arousal, but he moved with deliberate slowness, drawing out the moment until her excitement matched his.

"Ace." Her voice was breathless with need.

"Shh." He ran kisses across her shoulder, down her spine, and all the while his hands continued weaving their magic until her body was on fire.

He eased her thigh forward to allow smooth entry. And while he filled her, his fingers continued their exquisite manipulation, until she shuddered and cried out his name.

He turned her into his arms and their mouths mated

in a long slow kiss. Still locked in an embrace, they drifted back to sleep.

"What were we thinking?" Ally glanced at the bed-side clock and sat up, shoving the tangles from her eyes. "Ace, it's Monday. We have to get to work."

"Not yet." He lay wrapped in the sheets, one arm beneath his head. "Come back to bed."

She swung her legs to the floor. "You're insatiable."

"Yeah. Another vice I've only discovered since meeting you, Red."

She gathered up her kimono. "You can be as lazy as you please. I'm going to shower."

In the bathroom she hurried through her morning routine, pinning up her hair, brushing her teeth, before turning on the shower. Just as she stepped under the spray, she felt strong arms around her.

"Ace."

He drew her back against him and nibbled her shoul-der. "I got lonely in that big bed."

"So you came in here to scrub my back."

"Such a beautiful back."

She laughed and handed him a ball of netting filled with soap. "Here. Make yourself useful."

"What a waste of my talents, Red." He made sev-eral passes with the pouf. "What's this? Freckles." He lowered his mouth to her back. "How did I miss these all night? I love freckles." He pressed kisses to each of them, then slowly turned her until she was facing him. "Think I can find a few more of those?"

"When I was little, Gramps called them beauty spots."

"A smart man, your grandfather."

The spray plastered his hair to his neck as he trailed soapy kisses across her breasts, down her torso.

"Ace. You're going to make us both late for work."

"I can bend the rules. I'm the boss. Remember?"

She clutched his head. "Listen, boss, you've got to stop before we…"

Her words ended on a sudden moan of pleasure. And then, while the warm water played over them, they came together in a slow, delicious dance of love.

Chapter 10

"Well, Ace." Harlan rolled his scooter into the kitchen, pausing in the doorway to watch as Ace and Ally stood together by the stove, laughing over some shared secret. Seeing him they stepped apart. "I thought I'd heard your truck starting up early last evening."

"Yeah. I started to leave. But..." Ace cast a quick glance at Ally, then back to her grandfather. "I decided to spend the night. I hope you don't object?"

A smile played at the edges of Harlan's lips. "I may be old, but I can still remember what it felt like to be your age. As I recall, your head is ruled by your heart." He gave Ace a long, steady look. "So how's your heart feeling this morning?"

"Ready to burst. And strong as a bull. Right now I could lick the whole world. With one arm tied behind my back."

Harlan grinned, remembering perfectly the way that felt. "Is the coffee ready?"

"Yeah." Ace lifted the pot and filled three cups, then crossed the room and set one on the table.

"Ace." Ally spooned up something from the skillet. "Taste this and see if it's as good as yours."

He crossed to her, tasted, then smiled. "Perfect. My sister-in-law Maggie had better watch out, or you'll soon give her a run for her money."

"Not a chance." She filled three plates and carried them to the table. "Good morning, Gramps. Ready for some bacon and eggs?"

"Sounds great." The old man lifted his cheek for her morning kiss, then watched as Ace popped up the toast and carried it to the table.

Buster and Billy, who had danced in beside Harlan, stood watching Ally with soulful eyes.

"These two old fellas have been awfully jumpy all night, Allycat. I think they'd like to know they're forgiven for that mess they made."

Ally knelt down and caught Buster's big head between both her hands. "Yeah. I'll just bet you're sorry. Not because of the mess you made, but because of the tummyache you had to suffer afterward."

The dog peered at her so intently she had to laugh. "You know exactly what I'm saying, don't you?"

In reply he licked her hand.

"Okay. All is forgiven. I still love you." She ruffled his fur and offered her face for his quick kiss.

Billy danced around them, happy to see that he and his pal were back in her good graces. After several more loving licks, the two dogs settled down on either side of her.

Ace took his seat beside her and covered her hand

with his. "I knew you couldn't stay mad at these two old boys." With a laugh he leaned over to scratch their ears.

"You're as bad as they are." Ally squeezed his hand. "You've all got me figured for a soft touch."

"You are. And Buster and Billy and I are all glad of it."

It occurred to Harlan that these two looked as easy and comfortable as old lovers. He ought to feel uneasy about such a thing. But the truth was, they looked right together. This was a young man with a good heart. And his granddaughter deserved someone who would not only be good for her, but good to her as well.

"I've been thinking, Harlan." Ace took a helping of eggs. "Next time I'm in Prosperous, I'll pick up some materials to build a more permanent ramp for the front door."

"What's wrong with those timbers you already set in place? They do the job." Harlan slathered his toast with grape jelly.

"There's nothing wrong with them. But I intended them to be just a temporary fix, until I could come up with something better. I'll take some measurements and have the lumber company cut something to the exact size."

"You don't need to do that, Ace." Harlan sipped his coffee.

"I want to. And I've been thinking that you need a strip of asphalt from the house to the barn. That way, when it rains, your wheels won't sink in the mud."

"Asphalt." The old man shook his head. "Now you're talking hard work. I don't think that's something you could do by yourself."

Ace shrugged. "Maybe I could get my brothers to come over and give me a hand."

Harlan grinned across the table at his granddaughter, feeling oddly mellow. It was comforting to know that someone besides Ally might be here to lend a hand. The ranch and its problems had long ago gotten out of his control. And though he'd hated to admit it, they were certainly more than one woman, even one as single-minded as Ally, could handle alone.

There was just something about this young man that spoke of strength of character and depth of determination. Harlan had no doubt Ace would do whatever he said he would. In fact, the more he got to know Ace, the more he liked and trusted him.

He polished off the last of his eggs and sat back. "You know, Ace, you remind me a lot of myself when I was young."

"How so?" Ace sipped his coffee, enjoying the fact that Ally had her hand on his knee.

"I really believed I could do anything I set my mind to. I remember exploring the hills around here and thinking I ought to find a use for this land." He laughed. "It surely wasn't any good for raising cattle."

Ace smiled. "Pretty barren, all right. Not what you'd call good grazing land."

Harlan nodded. "I used to think maybe I'd hire a rig and take some soil samples."

"Why didn't you?"

Harlan sipped. Shrugged. "I just never followed through. I guess I was more of a dreamer than a doer. I dreamed of finding a fortune, so I could give up ranching. Then I dreamed of having my own studio, so I could just get away from my problems and be left alone to design my saddles." He shook his head. "But dreaming doesn't pay the bills."

"No." Ally topped off their cups. "But your saddles have paid plenty of bills in the past, Gramps." She turned to Ace. "He once had a Saudi prince offer him fifty thousand dollars for a saddle."

"A Saudi prince?" Ace looked impressed. "How did he hear about you?"

"He saw a saddle Gramps made for a movie star."

"Wait a minute." Ace held up his hand. "Back up here. Your grandfather made a saddle for a movie star?"

Ally nodded. "One of the old-time Hollywood cowboys. I've forgotten his name." She turned to her grandfather for confirmation.

"Zane Tyler. Owned half of Palm Springs at one time, I understand. He used to use that fancy saddle every year when he rode in the Rose Parade."

Ally picked up the story. "That's where the prince first saw it and tried to buy it. He wanted to use it for official celebrations in his country. But Zane Tyler wouldn't part with his for any amount of money, so that's when the prince decided to ask Gramps to make him one of his own." Ally's eyes were shining as she looked at her grandfather.

"Whew." Ace arched a brow. "You could get a lot of commissions with that kind of exposure. A movie star and royalty."

"There was a time when Gramps was known the world over for his saddles." Ally couldn't hide the note of pride in her voice.

"You could pay a lot of bills with that much profit. How long did it take you to make that saddle for the prince?"

"I didn't." Harlan set his cup down with a clatter.

"You didn't?"

Harlan pursed his lips. "That was at a low time in my life. I'd just been notified about the loss of my son. Ally was faraway and unable to leave her mother. I was struggling to run the ranch. There just wasn't time left over for anything else. So I told the prince I'd have to pass on his generous offer."

"Couldn't you have asked him to wait until you had the time?"

Harlan shrugged. "Maybe. I just didn't think of it. I simply sent my regrets and let it go at that."

"And after a while," Ally said softly, "the orders stopped coming in."

Harlan avoided his granddaughter's eyes. "You can't blame people. The way I dropped off the face of the earth, they probably think I'm dead."

Ace studied him. "You could take out an ad and let people know you're back."

"Yeah." Harlan pinched a hand over the bridge of his nose, as though fighting pain. "And I could discover gold on my property, too, son. But neither of those things is going to happen. So I'll go on making a couple of saddles a year, and hoping some local rancher comes up with enough money to buy them."

Ace could see that this conversation was disturbing to the old man. He got to his feet. "We'd better clean up this mess and think about getting to the mine."

Harlan looked up. "I don't believe I ever bothered to ask you. What do you do out at that mine, Ace?"

For a moment Ace thought he might be joking. When he realized the old man was serious he said, "I thought you knew. I own it."

Harlan chuckled. "Since when? Everybody knows that mine is owned by the Wilde family."

"Yeah." Ace deposited the dishes in the sink and turned. "That's me. Well..." He shrugged. "...My brothers and me."

"You're a Wilde?" Harlan's smile was gone. His eyes had gone dark and flat.

"That's right."

Harlan looked from Ace to his granddaughter. "Are you telling me that, knowing how I feel, you'd work for the Wildes?"

"I...needed a job, Gramps. Where else was I supposed to work?"

"Anywhere but for the Wildes." The old man slammed a hand down on the arm of his scooter. "And you." He fixed Ace with a look of fury. "How dare you take advantage of my hospitality? Not to mention the advantage you took of my granddaughter." He pointed a finger. "Get out of my house. Now. I don't ever want to see you around here again. Is that understood?"

"Gramps, please. Let me ex..."

"And you, girl." He rounded on her. "Letting a Wilde onto my property. Into my home. Get upstairs. Now. Before I say more than you want to hear."

Her eyes widened. In her entire life, she'd never seen her grandfather's temper aimed at her. Theirs had always been an idyllic relationship. "I'm not a child, Gramps. You can't send me up to bed with a lecture. We have to talk, as one adult to another."

"Oh, we'll talk all right. When this son of a..." He glared at Ace. "When this Wilde is off my property, you and I will talk. And not before."

Ace stood watching this scene with a look of complete disbelief. But the old man's anger was real. As was Ally's pain.

"I wanted to tell you last night, Gramps. I started to. But then Buster and Billy..."

"Not another word." Harlan pounded a fist on the table, sending silverware clattering to the floor. That had the dogs dropping into a crouch and backing away with matching looks of guilt. He pointed a finger. "Ace Wilde." He emphasized the last name with a sneer. "I want you out of my house right now. This minute. And don't you ever set foot on my property again."

"You have the right to order me out." Ace cautioned himself to hold his temper. Anything said in the heat of anger would only come back to haunt him later. "But I think you're making a big mistake if you turn this into a contest of love and ask your granddaughter to choose between the two of us."

The old man's face darkened with fury. "Are you so arrogant that you think I'd lose?" The words rang with contempt.

"No, sir." Ace glance toward Ally, who stood poised in the doorway, tears streaming down her cheeks. "It's just that, in a case like this, nobody can possibly win."

He crossed the room, pausing to touch a hand to her shoulder. He yearned to offer her some measure of comfort. Instead, he simply let himself out the door.

Minutes later his truck could be heard starting down the drive. And then there was only silence as an angry old man and a tearful young woman faced each other.

"I have good news and bad news." Thorpe's staccato voice on the telephone had Ace temporarily forgetting his temper.

"You've learned something?"

"You show a Marla Craine employed in your office."

Ace nodded wearily. "Yeah. I'm told she didn't show up for work today. And never even bothered to phone in sick." Just one more problem in a day that was slowly going downhill.

"Well." Thorpe's voice over the cellular phone faded in and out. "Don't expect her back. When we looked into her background, we learned that she was a close friend of your former assistant, Cassidy Kellerman. In fact, Marla was so close, she expected to be recommended as Ms. Kellerman's replacement. Upon further investigation we learned that she recently deposited a large sum of money in her bank account."

Ace's mind was racing. "You think somebody paid her in advance, hoping she'd be able to do some serious damage to WildeMining if she were to become my assistant?"

"That's a pretty good bet. When we went to see her over the weekend, she looked absolutely terrified by our questions. I suspected that she might try to run, so I assigned an operative to watch her. He just checked in from St. Louis. She caught a flight there yesterday, and is staying with an aunt."

"Now what?" Ace was suddenly alert. Maybe the whole day wasn't a wash.

"I think sooner or later Marla Craine will try to contact the person who paid her to sabotage your company, Mr. Wilde. And when she does that, we'll nail him."

"Thanks, Thorpe." Ace leaned back in his chair and smiled for the first time since morning. "I appreciate this. Keep me informed."

He disconnected and closed his eyes.

"Bad news?"

At the sound of that velvet voice, Ace's eyes snapped open. "Hey, Red." He got to his feet and stared at her with naked hunger. "Something tells me you didn't come here to ask for your job back."

She shook her head, avoiding his eyes. "You know I can't do that to Gramps. He's so hurt and angry. And it's all my fault. I should have told him who you were that first day, before he started to like you, and before I started to…" She bit her lip. There was no way now she could ever admit what was in her heart.

"Does he know you're here?"

She nodded. "I told him I just needed to collect my things." She felt the heat rise to her cheeks. "And my paycheck." Though it galled her to ask for money, she was desperate. Without this job, she and her grandfather had less than a month before the bills would begin piling up again.

Ace dialed a number. "Beth. Ace Wilde here. Cut a check for new employee Allison Brady. When it's ready, have someone bring it to my office."

"Well." She avoided looking at him. It was too painful. "I'll just clean out my desk."

While she filled her briefcase with her meager belongings, it occurred to Ally that this was the second time in less than a week that she was doing this. She felt tears sting her eyes and blinked them back. She wouldn't allow herself to cry over this. Couldn't. Because if she started, she'd never stop until she'd run out of tears.

She saw the young woman from accounting enter Ace's office and exit minutes later, and knew that her check was ready. There was nothing more to keep her here. She took a deep breath and walked into his office.

Without a word he handed her the check.

"I'm sorry, Ace."

"Yeah. Me, too." He watched as she folded the check and jammed it into her pocket. "Now what?"

She shrugged. "I don't know. I guess I'll drive over to Montana tomorrow and look for work. It won't be as interesting as this, but it'll keep my grandfather happy." She turned away with a sigh. "Oh, Ace, he's so hurt, so miserable, he actually called me Allison. He hasn't called me that since I was six years old and climbed up onto the back of a bull."

"You did what?" He caught her by the arm, then realized his mistake. The moment he touched her he felt the sizzle of heat that shot through his veins.

The only sign that she felt the same thing was a slight flush on her cheeks. "I climbed onto a bull's back and rode it halfway across the pasture before I was thrown."

"Why?"

"Because a boy in my class said girls couldn't do everything that boys could do. He said his big brother was a bull rider, and there weren't any girls who rode bulls in the rodeo. So I decided to show him he was wrong."

He felt the beginnings of a smile. "My kind of woman. I guess you showed him."

"Yeah. And then Gramps showed me the woodshed." She laughed as she rubbed her backside.

"And I'll bet he wanted to show you the woodshed again today. But he knows you're too old for that."

"Yeah. I guess. But not too old to feel terrible about misleading him."

He decided to discard whatever good intentions he'd made. He pulled her close and buried his face in her hair. And realized he couldn't let her go. Not without a fight.

"Come on." He caught her hand and started leading her toward the door.

"Where are we going?"

"To your grandfather's ranch. And this time, that old man's going to tell me what he and my father fought about all those years ago."

"What good will that do?"

"At least then I'll know how to make amends. How can I make it right when I don't even know what I'm fighting about?" Ignoring the employees in the outer office who were gaping at them, he continued holding her hand as he punched the button for the elevator. When they were downstairs, he led her toward his truck. "Come on. I'll drive."

"But what if the two of you don't resolve this? Maybe I'd better take my own truck."

"Uh-uh." He grinned. "This way, if all else fails, and he orders me off his property again, you'll have a good reason to come back to see me."

"So much dust," Ace muttered as they drove along the rutted path. "Like somebody just tore up this road going a hundred miles an hour." He turned to Ally. "Was your grandfather expecting a delivery truck?"

She shrugged. "Not that I know of."

As the ranch house came into view, both Ace and Ally fell silent. They both knew how much was riding on this one chance to appeal to Harlan Brady's sense of fair play. If the old man wanted to, he could simply refuse to give Ace an answer, and order him off the property.

As they drove closer, Ally sniffed the air. "Something's burning."

"Yeah." Ace's eyes narrowed at the pall of smoke rising above the trees. He pulled the truck into the dusty yard and turned toward the barn, where smoke was rising in a great black cloud.

Billy came rushing toward the truck, barking frantically.

"Gramps!" Ally was out of the truck before it came to a stop, with Ace directly behind her, and the little dog on his heels.

As they sprinted the distance between the house and barn, they suddenly caught sight of something that had them both stopping in their tracks.

"Oh, no. Oh, Gramps." Ally dropped to her knees beside the crumpled form of her grandfather, lying face down in the dirt. Close by was his scooter, which was now little more than a pile of twisted metal.

With sinking hearts she and Ace rolled Harlan over. When they heard him moan they sighed with relief.

"He's alive." Ally bent close, pressing her lips to his cheek. "Gramps, can you hear me?"

"Yeah…hear you." He lifted a hand to her face, then froze when he caught sight of Ace. "You did this."

"Gramps. Ace didn't do this. He was with me. Tell us what happened here."

"Ace knows." The old man's eyes flashed fire.

"I don't know, Harlan." Ace shot a puzzled glance toward Ally, wondering if her grandfather had lost his senses. "Tell us what happened here."

"A man. A stranger. Hauled me out of my workroom. Then he threw me down in the dirt and smashed the scooter, before setting fire to the barn."

Ace's eyes narrowed. "How did a stranger get past Buster?"

"Buster." A sigh seemed to well up from deep inside him. "That good old dog attacked him, trying to save me."

"And?" Ally waited, her heart pounding.

The old man's eyes filled and his lips trembled. "He shot Buster."

Ace was already on his feet, racing toward the barn. The fire had spread from the workroom to the bedroom beyond. He ran through a wall of flame and watched as charred timbers crashed to the floor in a display of fireworks.

Ace spotted the still figure of the old dog and lifted him, staggering under the deadweight. Just as he stepped outside more timbers crashed and burned, and a wall of the barn exploded inward, sending up a billowing cloud of smoke and sparks.

Ace gently lay the old dog down beside Ally and her grandfather, who clung together, weeping softly.

The sight of Buster brought a fresh round of weeping from Ally, who turned and buried her face in the old dog's ruff.

"He isn't dead." Ace's eyes narrowed. "But he's badly wounded." He turned to Harlan. "This stranger had to say something. Didn't he tell you why he was here and what this was all about?"

"He told me." Harlan's eyes were dark with hatred. "He said he was delivering a message from the Wildes. That they never forget. And they never forgive. And this was their way of collecting on an old debt."

Chapter 11

"All right." His eyes hot with fury, Ace got to his feet. "I don't know how yet, but we're going to get to the bottom of this."

"You're going to get off my property." Despite his injuries, Harlan's voice quivered with anger.

"That's right. I am. And you're going with me." Ace picked up the old man and, ignoring his furious protest, carried him to the truck, where he deposited him inside. Then he returned to where Buster lay, still and silent as death.

"Get some blankets from the house," he called as he picked up the old dog. At once Billy started dancing around his legs, yapping wildly.

By the time Ace carried the old dog to his truck, Ally had returned with several blankets.

"Climb up here, Red." He helped her into the back of the truck.

When she was seated with her back against the cab,

he wrapped the dog in the blankets and settled him on Ally's lap. Poor old Billy danced around the truck, barking in protest. As soon as Ace lifted him up he raced to Ally's side. Finding Buster there, he settled down, his head beside that of his pal.

Finally Ace retrieved the broken scooter, tying it down in the back of the truck so it wouldn't roll around. Then he paused to squeeze Ally's shoulder.

"Hang on. And hold a good thought. He's a tough old dog. Almost as tough as that grandfather of yours. They're both going to be fine."

Then he climbed into the truck and turned on the key. With the wheels spewing gravel, he turned away from the pall of smoke that filled the air, and the burning rubble that had once been Harlan's workroom and barn, and headed toward home. And prayed they'd all make it alive.

"What's this?" Harlan watched as the graceful soaring roofline of the Double W came into view.

Ace disconnected his cell phone and lowered it to his pocket. "I'm taking you to my place."

"You young fool." The air nearly turned blue with a string of vicious oaths. "What do I have to do to make you understand? I want nothing to do with you and your family. Nothing."

"Yeah. You've made that pretty clear. But right now you don't have a choice. That old dog needs help. And my brother Hazard is the best vet in the county."

"A vet? Your brother is a vet?" His tone revealed that he'd expected all the Wildes to be thieves and villains.

"That's what I said. And if anybody can save old

Buster, it's Hazard. I've already alerted him that we're coming, and he's standing by.''

They rolled to a stop at the back door and Ace was relieved to see Hazard just stepping out onto the porch.

''Here's your patient.'' Ace leapt from the truck and hurried to Ally's side, where she cradled the old dog. Her cheeks were wet with tears. ''He's been shot.''

Hazard took the blanket-clad burden from her arms as gently as if it were an infant. ''I'll want you beside him, Ally. It'll soothe him to feel your touch, and hear your voice, at least until he's under anesthesia.''

She nodded and scrambled out of the truck to follow him inside.

Ace picked up Billy and carried him to Harlan. The old man took the little dog without a word. Then Ace returned to the back of the truck and hauled the twisted metal to the barn.

Cody looked up as he entered.

''Think you can get this thing running?''

The old cowboy scratched his head. ''I can try.''

''That's all I ask.''

Ace strode back to the truck and climbed inside before turning to Harlan, who was holding tightly to the little dog. ''Now I'll drive you into Prosperous.''

''What for?'' Harlan demanded.

''So a doctor can look at those injuries.''

''Don't need any fool doctor looking at me. I'm just cut up is all. Right now I'm more worried about Buster.''

''I told you. He'll get the best care possible.''

''That's what you say.'' The old man's chin jutted in the same way Ally's did when she was angry. ''I'm not going anywhere until I see for myself that he's all right.''

"Okay. Suit yourself. But you'll be stuck spending time in the enemy camp." Ace turned off the key and slammed out of the truck. Obstinate old man, he thought, as he came around and opened the passenger door. Without a word he lifted Harlan, still clinging to his dog, and carried him up the steps and into the house.

With Agnes and Maggie watching in openmouthed surprise, he strode through the kitchen and made his way to the great room, depositing his burden on a sofa.

"I'll get some soap and water and disinfectant for those cuts," Ace muttered as he walked away.

When he was alone Harlan leaned his head back and closed his eyes, exhausted by his ordeal. When Ace returned he found the old man asleep, with the little dog still cuddled in his arms. He watched for a few moments, then set aside the basin of water and clean cloths. He'd tend the old man's wounds later. For now, he'd let him rest.

"He's going to be all right. I just know it." Erin had her arm around Ally's shoulder as she led her from the lab, where Hazard had set up his surgery. "I've seen my husband work miracles with injured animals."

"I know. But Buster is so old." Ally's lips quivered, and when she spotted Ace, she flew into his arms and buried her face in his chest. "Oh, Ace. What if he doesn't…"

"Shh." He pressed his lips to her temple. "Hang on, Red. Hold a good thought."

"I'm trying." He could feel the tremors that shook her. "But he was so still. So quiet."

"I know. But I know this, too. If anybody can save that old dog, Hazard can."

Erin stood across the room watching. If anyone had told her, just one week ago, that her wild and reckless brother-in-law would be the calm in the eye of a hurricane, she'd have scoffed. But here he was, steady as a rock, while those around him were falling apart.

From his position on the sofa, Harlan Brady was watching as well. And resenting every moment that his granddaughter was being held by the son of his enemy.

He cleared his throat, and she turned, then crossed the room to kneel at his feet. "You okay, Gramps?"

"I'm fine."

"You're bleeding all over your shirt."

"I am?" He seemed surprised as he glanced down at himself.

"Yes. And all over Billy." She took the little dog from his arms and buried her face in his fur. And began to silently weep.

Harlan lay a hand on her head, feeling completely helpless. And hating it. His voice was gruff. "Stop your crying, Allycat. He'll be fine. He's tough."

"I know." She lifted her head and forced a smile through her tears.

Just then Hazard stepped into the room and surveyed the scene. "I was able to remove the bullet. It didn't hit any vital organs. But he's lost a lot of blood. The next twenty-four hours will be critical. Erin and I will take turns sitting with him." As he stepped closer he saw the blood on the old man's face. "You need to see a doctor. You may need stitches for that cut."

"He won't go," Ace said from across the room.

"Your brother bragged that you're the best vet in the county. If you're as good as he claims, why can't you stitch me up?" Harlan demanded.

Hazard stared at the old man for several moments

before coming to a decision. "Okay. I can take a look. But I warn you, if I find anything serious, I'll have Ace haul your hide into Prosperous, or we'll fly you up to the hospital in Laramie."

"You won't do either one." Harlan's chin lifted like a prizefighter. "Just clean me up and stitch what you have to. That's as much doctoring as I'll allow."

Hazard left the room and returned with his medical bag. With Erin assisting, the old man's injuries were cleaned and disinfected, and several gaping cuts were stitched.

Hazard studied the old man, who hadn't made so much as a whimper during the entire procedure. "I'm going to give you something for pain."

Harlan held up a hand. "Don't want anything that's going to make me feel all fuzzy-brained."

"All you'll do is sleep for a couple of hours. When you wake up, your mind will be clear. I promise." Hazard handed him two pills and a glass of water.

Reluctantly the old man swallowed them. Minutes later, Agnes shuffled into the room with a pillow and blanket. Harlan Brady offered no protest when his granddaughter plumped the pillow and eased him down before covering him with a blanket.

With his legs draped over the end of the sofa, he slept.

"And this stranger, who beat up the old man and shot his dog before torching the barn, said he was sent there by us?" Chance and Hazard confronted Ace in the library of their home, which they used as an office. It was the one room where they could count on being undisturbed.

Chance sat behind the desk. Hazard sank into a chair

on the opposite side of the desk, while Ace paced nervously to the window and back.

"That's what Harlan claims." Ace shook his head. "I know it sounds incredible. But even though he hates us I can't imagine he'd make up such a story." He paused and turned toward his brothers. "I'll tell you something. When I saw that fire and that old dog lying bleeding in the middle of it, I realized someone had a real grudge against Harlan Brady. I knew I had to get him and Ally out of there right away."

"Wait a minute. Back up." Chance held out a hand. "What were you doing there in the first place? Especially in the middle of the day. Why weren't you working?"

"Okay." Ace slumped down into a chair. "To start with, Harlan Brady found out my name and ordered me off his property."

"When was this?" Chance demanded.

"This morning."

His two brothers glanced at each other.

"This morning." Hazard cleared his throat. "And where did you spend last night?"

"At the Brady place. With Ally."

Hazard turned to Chance. "And all this time we thought business was so good at the mine that he was sleeping there. We should have known. Wherever there's a pretty face and a killer body, little brother can't be far away."

"Listen." Ace lunged forward, catching the front of his brother's shirt and dragging him close. "Ally's not just a face and a body. Got that?"

"Yeah. Sure." Hazard slapped his hand away and straightened his shirt. "And I didn't just hear you say you'd slept with her."

"Don't say it like that."

"Why not? Isn't that what you just told us?"

"Yeah. But you make it sound like...a one-night stand."

"Oh. You mean you're going to defy the old man and sleep with her again?"

"See?" Ace caught him in a vicious grip, this time holding a fist to his face. "You keep twisting my words. It isn't like that with Ally. She's different."

"Oh, yeah." Chance rounded the desk and stepped between them. "We can see that she's different. Really a hag. Ugly face. No body to speak of."

"Very funny." Ace shoved him hard enough to send him crashing against the wall. "That's enough, Chance."

"Uh-uh." His oldest brother came at him with both fists, and managed to catch him with an uppercut that sent him spinning. "You started this. Now let's see you finish it."

"You want an ending?" Ace butted his head into Chance's midsection, dropping him to his knees. "Here's your ending. Ally's something special."

Hazard's jaw dropped. "You mean like a wife?"

"Of course not." Ace nearly choked. "I just mean... Hell, I don't know what I mean. But she's special. And don't you forget it." He turned to Hazard, and landed a punch to his nose, sending blood spurting.

"Oh, you're going to pay for that. You dump our father's enemy in our laps, and tell us you're goo-goo-eyed over his granddaughter, and expect us to just swallow this swill." Hazard returned punch for punch, until both brothers were bruised and bloody, and struggling for breath.

"I'm with Hazard." Chance stepped between them.

"Time for you to straighten out this mess, little brother. You caused it. You clean it up. And I suggest you start by finding out just what the hell was between Dad and Harlan Brady. And, by the way, this one's for that head butt," he muttered as he landed a solid blow to Ace's chin, driving him back against the door.

When he straightened, the door opened and Maggie stood on the threshold.

"Oh, good. I just love it when the three of you get together for one of your manly talks." She stood surveying the damage, hands on her hips. Then she turned to her husband. "Dinner is ready. I hope you'll clean up that blood before you come to the table." She turned to the other two. "And, in case you're interested, Hazard, Erin says your patient is awake and starting to howl. And Ace, Ally says her grandfather is making noises about crawling home if someone doesn't volunteer to drive him soon." She walked away, muttering under her breath about there never being a dull moment in the Wilde household.

Chance offered a hand to Ace, helping him to his feet. "You all right?"

Ace shook his head to clear it. "Yeah. I guess so."

"Good. You'd better see if you can talk some sense into that nasty old man." Chance turned to Hazard. "And you'd better hope that patient of yours lives. Otherwise, I have a notion that Harlan Brady will probably be seeing a lawyer and saying you caused his old dog's death."

Ace paused. "I like what you said about finding out what went on between Dad and Harlan Brady. The only trouble is, of the two who know the truth, one is dead, and the other refuses to talk about it."

"Then I suggest you use some of that charm, little

bro.'' Chance punched his arm. ''Because unless you solve the mystery of Harlan's hatred of the Wildes, your future with his granddaughter doesn't look very bright.''

The three brothers walked from the library, arms around each other's shoulders, feeling almost euphoric. There was nothing like a good knock-down-drag-out fight to clear the air. Except maybe a good meal, followed by a night of good loving.

''Where's that son of a…?'' When Ace ambled into the room, Harlan's lips peeled back in a snarl that resembled his dog's. ''I've spent all the time I intend to in this house.''

''Gramps.'' Ally hurried over to clasp his hands in hers. ''You've been asleep for almost three hours now. You can't just up and leave.''

''Why can't I?''

Her mind raced. She'd had plenty of time to talk over her dilemma with Ace and his family. They were all convinced that, for the sake of safety, she and her grandfather needed to remain here. But she knew that no matter how carefully she couched her words, Harlan Brady would resist the idea of staying even one night under their roof. So she carefully avoided talking about anything except the most mundane things.

''First of all, because Maggie has dinner ready. It wouldn't be polite to leave without accepting her hospitality.''

His eyes narrowed on Ace, who remained across the room. ''I'm not interested in being polite to a Wilde.''

''Your fight isn't with Maggie.''

''She's a Wilde, isn't she?'' He looked around, wishing he could see something he could lean on. ''You go find me something with wheels, so I can get out of here.''

Ace stepped closer. "Cody's fixing your scooter. If anyone can make it work again, it's him."

"I'm not hanging around for any mangled scooter. Just get me something to lean on."

"Okay." Ace strolled away, leaving Ally watching in stunned silence. Why had he given in so easily?

"You stay here, Gramps," she said foolishly, knowing the old man couldn't get himself across the room without help.

When she reached the kitchen she stopped. Ace had the door between the two rooms open and was fanning the air with a towel. "What in the world are you doing?"

"Seeing that that stubborn old man gets a whiff of Maggie's pot roast."

Ally started laughing. "Spoken like a man."

"It takes one to know one. No matter how eager he is to leave, I don't think any red-blooded man can resist Maggie's cooking." He continued fanning the air.

A few minutes later he returned to the great room, where Harlan sat scowling. "I'll arrange for somebody to drive you home right after supper." He kept his smile in place. "Don't know if you're interested in joining us. Maggie's made pot roast. Ally said she may as well have some, since the truck and driver won't be ready for another hour or two."

Harlan pressed his lips together. But from this distance, Ace could see the old man breathing deeply.

"Pot roast, huh?"

"Yeah. Smothered in gravy. With new potatoes and carrots and beans from her garden. Maggie grows all these fancy herbs, too. Taste amazing in pot roast." He started to turn away, then paused. ''I could take you to the kitchen, if you'd like to join us.''

Harlan held back for almost a full minute before giving a grudging nod of his head. ''I suppose I could eat a little something.''

Ace sauntered across the room and picked him up, then carried him to the kitchen, where he settled him on a chair at the table. Billy trailed behind and lay down beside his master.

The others were already there.

''I'm glad you could join us.'' Maggie removed flaky rolls from the oven and arranged them in a basket.

Harlan watched in silence as she carried a platter to the table and began to carve thick slices of beef so tender it nearly fell off the bone. She served his plate, adding potatoes and vegetables. From a fancy dish with a ladle she poured gravy that was as smooth as silk. The aroma in this kitchen was enough to make a man drool.

Cody entered, hanging his hat by the door and taking his place beside Harlan.

Harlan looked up. ''I hear you're fixing my scooter.''

Cody nodded. ''Trying to. Pretty busted up. But I think I'll have it up and running by tomorrow.''

''I'm obliged.'' The words nearly choked him. Though he had no grudge against this cowboy, there was no doubt his loyalty lay with the Wildes. That made him an enemy in Harlan's eyes. ''I'll have my granddaughter drive over to fetch it when it's ready.''

Ally glanced around, assuming someone would voice a protest over his planned departure. Instead, the others went on eating.

Harlan managed to clean his plate twice, along with

a generous slice of home-baked apple pie and two cups of fresh-ground coffee. When he finally sat back, he could feel his strength returning.

He turned to Maggie. "I guess when it comes to cooking, your brother-in-law doesn't exaggerate. That was one fine meal, ma'am."

"Thank you, Harlan. I'm glad you enjoyed it."

"I did. And now," he said, turning to Ace, who was still sipping his coffee, "I'd appreciate that ride home."

To Ally's surprise, Ace nodded. "I'll get my keys."

Before he could get to his feet Hazard stopped him. "I'm puzzled, Harlan. Don't you care about Buster?"

"Buster?" The old man leaned forward. "What about him? My granddaughter told me he came through the surgery without a problem."

"He did. But he has a long way to go before he's fully recovered. He's bound to wake every few hours. And when he does, he's going to need to see a familiar face. Otherwise, his old heart might not take the shock of being in a strange place, with strange people."

Harlan's brow wrinkled with concern, as he digested the information in silence. "Then we'll take Buster home with us. I've had dogs all my life. I've learned a thing or two about taking care of them."

"But this is special, Gramps." Ally squeezed his hand. "Buster's been shot. Hazard is giving him antibiotics intravenously. We could never do that at home."

Harlan turned to Hazard. "Will you let me at least see him?"

"I'll do better than that." Hazard glanced toward his wife. "Erin and I thought you might want to sleep in my lab tonight. We've fixed a cot beside Buster's cage. That way, whenever he wakes, he'll see you and smell you and be comforted by your presence. If you sense that he's in any trouble, there's a bell beside the cot. Just ring it and I'll be there in seconds.'' He leaned down to pet the little dog who lay at Harlan's feet. ''You and Billy will play an important part in Buster's healing.''

Harlan studied him a moment before nodding. ''Ace said you were the finest vet in the county. I can see why. You don't see your patients as just dumb animals.''

''There's no such thing as a dumb animal. They speak to us in a dozen different ways.'' He met the old man's look. ''How about going to see Buster now?''

Harlan nodded.

Ace winked at Ally before lifting her grandfather in his arms and carrying him easily from the room. It hadn't been nearly as difficult as he'd feared. Of course, while the old man slept, Ace and his brothers had discussed every possible argument they could use. And all three had agreed that his love for his old dog would be the most compelling.

At least, for tonight, they'd won a reprieve. But knowing the old man's temper, they'd have to unravel this mystery quickly. Harlan Brady wouldn't be willing to stay under their roof one day longer than was absolutely necessary.

Chapter 12

"Gramps." Ally, fresh from her morning shower, hurried across the room to where her grandfather sat on the edge of his bunk, running a hand over Buster's head.

Ace remained in the doorway, unwilling to intrude on the old man's apparent happiness. It was bad enough that he'd spent the night in Ally's arms. He didn't want to appear to be gloating in front of her grandfather.

"How's our old boy?" Ally knelt beside the cage and joined her hand to Harlan's, smoothing, stroking the dog's scorched fur.

"He woke up a couple of times through the night. Started howling until he saw me and Billy. That seemed to settle him down."

"Poor old thing." She smiled at her grandfather. "Aren't you glad you stayed?"

"Yeah." He glanced at the man in the doorway, then back at his granddaughter. "Where'd you sleep?"

"In the guest room." She flushed at his scrutiny and was relieved to see Hazard and Erin just coming in to check on their patient.

"How did Buster do last night?" Hazard asked.

"You were right. He woke up howling a couple of times. But he settled right down when he saw me." Harlan glanced up. "I hope you don't mind. I let Billy sleep beside him in the cage."

"Good idea." Hazard knelt and checked Buster's vital signs, then straightened. "His heartbeat's stronger. His breathing easier." He shook his head. "That's one tough old dog. I think, barring any complications, he's going to be just fine."

"When can I take him home?" Harlan watched as Hazard prepared a fresh intravenous solution.

"Let's keep a close eye on him today. That'll give me a better idea of just how soon he can be turned loose."

"Fair enough." Harlan sank back on his cot. When he saw his granddaughter's look of alarm he gave her a quick, reassuring smile. "Guess maybe I need another day myself. Not as strong as I thought I was."

"You take all the time you need." Hazard sat on the edge of the cot and took the old man's pulse. Satisfied, he stood. "Nothing wrong that a little rest won't cure. Why don't I have your breakfast brought in here? That way you and Buster and Billy can have some quiet time together."

"I'd like that. Thanks." Harlan squeezed his granddaughter's hand. "You go have your breakfast with the others, Allycat. I think maybe I'll just snooze for a while."

"All right." She nodded toward the bell. "If you need me, just ring."

"I will." He closed his eyes.

Ally watched him a few moments, before following Hazard from the lab. In the doorway she stepped into Ace's arms, and gave a long, deep sigh.

Ace gathered her close to press a kiss to her cheek. "They're both going to be just fine, Red."

"I know. But I worry."

"Yeah. So we'll worry together. Come on. Let me feed you."

Behind them the old man watched from beneath lowered lids. They had just confirmed his worst fears. Despite all his warnings, nothing had changed between Ace Wilde and his granddaughter.

He turned away and, pushing aside his agitation, managed to drift back to sleep.

"I should be going to work with you." Ally stood on the porch beside Ace. Breakfast had been a hurried affair, with the three brothers scattering in three different directions immediately afterward. Chance had flown off to Laramie. Hazard had driven off in a truck with a group of wranglers. Already the helicopter sat idling on a pad a short distance from the house, its blades spinning, awaiting Ace. "I hate seeing you going alone."

"Yeah." Ace nibbled the corner of her mouth. "I hate it, too. If I had you up at the mine, I could lock my office door and have my way with you."

She laughed. "You did that last night."

"So I did." He gave her one of his heart-stopping grins. "Well, at least I'll manage to get some work done without all those distractions I have to fight when you're around." He gave her a quick, hard kiss. "See that your grandfather stays put."

"I'll try. But you know Gramps."

"Yeah." He shook his head.

But as he walked away Ace realized that was part of his problem. He didn't really know Harlan Brady at all. Yet. But he intended to. He intended to learn all he could about the man and the cause of the grudge he was still nursing after all these years.

Minutes later, as the helicopter skimmed the fields dark with cattle, Ace held the cell phone to his ear and strained to hear above the roar of the engines. "Thorpe? Anything new on Marla Craine?"

He listened, frowned, then shouted, "All right. Stay on it. Sooner or later she has to make a move. Now, I have another job for you. This one has to do with my father, and a man named Harlan Brady. I need to know what happened between them years ago. See what you can dig up. And Thorpe?" He paused. "I know I'm sending you off in a lot of different directions, but I'd appreciate whatever speed you can put on this."

When he rang off he dropped the phone into his pocket, then slipped on his sunglasses and stared out the window. The sight of this vast stretch of land never failed to stir him. But today he was unmoved as he saw, in his mind's eye, something else. The pall of smoke. The roar of flame. And one old man, battered and defenseless, staring at him with a look of horror and revulsion. Harlan Brady's fear and loathing weren't fake. The damage done to him was real, as was the danger that still existed somewhere out there.

Someone was going to great lengths to make the Wilde family look like selfish monsters. But who? Why? Who could possibly benefit from such a lie?

Agitated, Ace tapped a hand on the briefcase beside him, then he suddenly plucked the cell phone from his pocket and punched in a series of numbers.

Hearing Cody's voice he said, "Where are you?"

"In the barn. Working on that scooter."

"How's it going?"

"Okay. I think I'll be able to get it running today."

"Good. Cody, I want you to stick close to the house today."

There was the slightest pause. "Any particular reason?"

Ace fought to keep his tone even. "I'd just feel better knowing you're keeping an eye on…things."

The old cowboy cleared his throat. "Agnes has some repairs she wants made around the place. This might be a good day to see to them."

"Thanks, Cody. I appreciate it. I'll be home early."

He rang off and continued staring out the window. When the helicopter landed at the mine, he leapt clear of the craft and headed toward his office, deep in thought.

"So, Ally, tell us." Maggie looked up from the sink. "Are you really a better pool player than Ace?"

The two sisters-in-law had spent the better part of the afternoon in the kitchen with Ally. Maggie was baking bread, one of her passions. She had put Erin to work at the sink, washing the fresh vegetables she'd picked from her small garden beside the barn. And Ally was loading into the dishwasher the plate, bowl and utensils she'd just hauled from the lab, where her grandfather had enjoyed a late lunch. She was concerned about his lack of appetite.

"Ace is good. No doubt about it." Ally separated the silverware and stowed it in the basket.

"But you think you're better?" Maggie checked the oven temperature before placing the pan of dough on the rack.

Ally shrugged. "It's hard to say. The first time we played, I had the advantage."

"Why?" Both women looked up with interest.

"Because he didn't know I could even play the game. He was so busy being dazzled, he wasn't really giving a thought to winning. He was just trying not to beat me too badly."

"Poor Ace." Maggie couldn't help giggling. "He's always been so proud of the fact that he's a hustler. It had to be humiliating to be beaten at his own game. And by a woman."

"Yeah." Ally dried her hands on a kitchen towel. "I really took unfair advantage wherever I could."

"How?" Erin paused in her work to look over.

"By batting my lashes and acting so...helpless. Guys just eat that up."

Erin shook her head. "Just think of all the things I've been denied."

Ally looked puzzled. "What does that mean?"

Maggie giggled again. "Erin led a very sheltered life before coming from Boston to Wyoming. She had actually never even flirted with a guy before Hazard."

Ally stared at her in surprise. "You're kidding."

"No." Erin shared a smile with her sister-in-law. "Maggie's telling you the truth. I really had no clue. I guess that's one of the things Hazard loved about me."

"Yeah. What guy wouldn't?" Ally studied her more closely. "How are you adjusting to life in Wyoming?"

"I'm thriving." Erin set out the clean vegetables on

layers of paper toweling as precisely as she handled the instruments in her laboratory. "I've even learned to wear jeans and boots, and Hazard is teaching me to ride horseback." She saw the smile of pleasure on Ally's face. "I take it you like to ride?"

"I love it. I'm as comfortable in the saddle as I am in my grandfather's old truck."

"Then you're glad to be back in Wyoming?"

"Oh, you can't imagine." Ally looked up as the kettle whistled, and Maggie filled a teapot with boiling water. Soon the three women were sitting at the kitchen table, sipping tea. "I went to college in Minneapolis. That's where my mother settled after my father left us to work on an oil rig in the Atlantic. I was eleven years old, and I hated every day that I was separated from my grandfather. Throughout my entire childhood, he had been my best friend. I kept telling myself it would only be for a year or two. But the years stretched out into more than fifteen. And in all that time, I never stopped yearning to be back with Gramps. It didn't matter that his place wasn't much of a ranch, or that he wasn't much of a rancher. All that mattered was that we'd be together again."

"What took you so long?" Maggie asked gently.

"My mother. She was alone, and in very frail health, and absolutely determined to never return to life on a ranch. She'd hated it. And as much as I yearned for it, I was all the family she had." She sipped, then set her cup down, staring into the amber liquid. "And now I'm the only family Gramps has. And I'm being asked to put my own life on hold all over again, for the sake of someone else's."

Maggie and Erin exchanged a look.

Maggie put a hand over Ally's. "Don't give up hope

yet, Ally. Erin and I have learned that the Wilde brothers are very determined when they want something. And from the look on Ace's face, I'd say he has no intention of giving you up without a fight."

"Oh, Maggie," she whispered fervently. "I hope you're right."

The three women looked up at the sound of a bell being rung from the lab. Agnes scurried in from the other room, muttering under her breath.

"No need to worry about your grandfather. I can tell he's feeling as good as new."

Ally arched a brow. "How can you tell, Agnes?"

"Hear that bell? When a man starts demanding another glass of water, and another pillow, it's a sure sign he's got nothing better to do. Between him and that bell, and Cody underfoot all day fixing things, I may have to commit murder and mayhem."

While the others chuckled, Ally touched a hand to the old woman's arm. "I'll go see what my grandfather wants."

"It's my job," Agnes protested.

"You didn't ask for this. My grandfather and I have created too much extra work for you. You sit down and have a nice cup of tea. I'll see to him."

As she rushed from the room, the old housekeeper stared after her. "Huh. She thinks I don't know what she's up to."

Maggie retrieved another cup and saucer and returned to the table. "What is she up to, Agnes?"

"Trying to soften me up, that's what."

"Why?"

"Because I saw Ace coming out of her room this morning. Looking like the cat that swallowed the canary. Poor boy doesn't have any idea what kind of trap's being set for him. But I know. And she knows I know. Women have an instinct for that kind of thing.''

Maggie arched a brow. ''What kind of thing?''

''She's after my boy.''

Maggie and Erin refused to look at one another, knowing if they did they'd burst into gales of laughter. Instead Erin covered her mouth with her napkin, while Maggie busied herself pouring tea.

Both women were remembering their own cool receptions by this woman who had appointed herself the defender of ''her boys.'' But there was simply no help for it. Ally would have to find her own way into Agnes's good graces.

''Look, Allycat.'' Harlan turned to the old dog in the cage. ''Come on, boy.'' He beamed with pride as Buster stood and took two tentative steps before sitting back on his haunches.

''Oh, Gramps. That's just wonderful.'' Ally hugged him, then knelt down and petted the dog's head.

Buster rewarded her with a lick of his tongue across her hand before dropping his head on his paws.

''If he keeps this up, we ought to be able to leave here by tomorrow.''

''Let's leave that up to Hazard, Gramps.''

He seemed about to argue, when he heard the sound of the helicopter overhead. His eyes narrowed as he watched Ally race to the window to watch it land.

Minutes later Ace strode into the lab, followed by Cody, riding in the scooter.

''Look at this.'' Ace paused, allowing Cody to edge past him and come to a stop next to Harlan's cot.

''You fixed it?''

''Good as new.'' Cody stepped off and motioned for Harlan to climb aboard. ''Give it a try.''

Harlan eased himself from the cot to the scooter. With a simple touch of the button he was skimming around the lab. By the time he brought it to a stop beside Cody, he was smiling. ''I really thought it was beyond repair.'' He shook his head. ''You're a miracle worker.''

''That's what I told him when he fixed our old truck, Gramps.''

''It was Cody who fixed it?''

She nodded.

Harlan hesitated for several seconds, then stuck out his hand. ''Then I thank you. Twice.''

Cody held back, wiping his palm on his jeans, before accepting his handshake. ''I'm happy I could help.''

To ease the awkwardness between them, Ace knelt down beside Buster's cage. ''How's our old patient to-day?''

In reply, Buster eased himself up and took a step closer, sniffing Ace's outstretched hand before licking it. Following his lead, Billy hurled himself into Ace's arms and licked his face.

''You've had quite a scare, haven't you old boy?'' Ace picked up the little dog and scratched its ears. ''You figured you'd lost your best friend?''

Billy gave a yip of agreement.

Even Harlan found himself smiling at the dog's antics.

When Ace knelt down and released him, Billy crawled into the cage to cuddle up beside Buster.

The others looked up when Agnes paused in the doorway. ''Maggie said dinner's ready.'' She stared at

Harlan. "She wants to know if you want yours in here."

Harlan was about to nod his head when he saw Ace lower a hand to Ally's shoulder and whisper in her ear. At once his spine stiffened. "Now that I've got my wheels, I guess I'll just go along with everybody else to the kitchen."

Agnes walked away smiling. She'd just been spared another chore.

Behind her, Harlan steered his scooter along the hallway, while Cody trailed behind.

As Ally started to follow, Ace drew her back and closed the door to the lab.

"What are you doing? You heard Agnes. Maggie has dinner ready."

"Yeah." He framed her face with his hands and brushed his lips over hers. "But first, give me the welcome I've been waiting for all day."

At once the spark leapt between them, and she twined her arms around his neck, drawing him closer.

"Oh, Red." He kissed her slowly, savoring her lips as though they tasted of the most exotic flavors in the world. "This was definitely worth waiting for."

Minutes later, as the heat rose between them, Ally lifted her head and dragged air into her lungs. "Ace. We can't do this. We'll be missed."

"Yeah." He pressed his forehead to hers and struggled to bank the fire. "That's the trouble with sharing a house with this big family. There's never any time for...appetizers."

She smiled and kissed the tip of his nose. "Don't worry. I have something special saved for...dessert."

He threw back his head and roared. "You see? That's one more reason why I love you, Red." He wrapped an arm around her shoulders and opened the door, before walking with her toward the kitchen.

As she moved beside him she thought about the word he'd just spoken so lightly. Love. Did he mean it? Or was this handsome charmer so used to saying such things, they just spilled from his lips without thinking?

All afternoon Maggie and Erin had regaled her with stories from his wild and reckless youth. He'd given his brothers too many heart-stopping moments. But from what she'd heard, they never held such things against him. In fact, they loved him without reservation. And his sisters-in-law adored him. As for Agnes, she'd made her position abundantly clear. Ace was hers. The youngest of the three she'd been tending since they were motherless boys.

Was that why she loved him, as well? Ally nearly stumbled as the thought struck her. She wasn't just in love. She loved. Completely. Desperately.

"Hey. What's wrong?" Ace's hand tightened at her shoulder, and he drew her close against him.

"Nothing." She felt oddly breathless. Her heart racing, her palms sweating at the sudden realization. She did love him. For the patience he showed to her grandfather. For the cool, competent way he'd taken charge when their world around them seemed to be spinning out of control. And for the tenderness he'd shown an ornery old dog. But it was more than all that. She just simply loved him. Because of himself. She loved his humor. His strength. His honor.

They paused before stepping into the kitchen and Ace glanced down at her with a puzzled expression. "You sure you're okay?"

"Oh, Ace. I'm more than okay. I feel so happy."

She stood on tiptoe and pressed a quick kiss to his mouth.

"What was that for?"

"Because I wanted to." She started to turn away and he caught her arm, drawing her close. Her eyes widened. "Now what?"

"Red, I just want you to know…" His voice was so serious, she had a moment of fear. Then she saw the way his lips curved. "…Any time you want to kiss me, I'm willing to sacrifice these lips. In fact, if you'd like, I'm willing to sacrifice this entire body."

"Save it, cowboy." She started into the kitchen, then muttered under her breath, "At least until dessert."

They were both grinning like conspirators as they took their places at the table alongside the others.

Chapter 13

" . . . So there we were, struggling to pay back taxes, and Ace announced that he'd just sunk us into more debt by hiring a soil-boring company." Hazard shook his head and laughed. He and Chance had spent the entire dinner hour regaling Ally with stories about Ace's youthful misadventures.

Through the entire narrative, Harlan Brady had remained silent, watching and listening. Now he couldn't hold back. "Are you telling me you had no idea that there was coal and uranium on your property?"

"How could we have known that?" Hazard helped himself to another slice of prime beef, then added more vegetables. "I was so busy worrying about scraping up enough money to keep from losing the Double W, I didn't have time to dream." He glanced around the table. "I left the dreaming to Chance and Ace. And believe me, their dreams have paid off. But at the time, we were just green kids, and all those dreams seemed like so much smoke.''

Chance saw the puzzled look on Harlan's face. ''Something bothering you, Harlan?''

The old man ducked his head. ''Just wondering what happened to all that money your old man was supposed to have.''

''Money?'' Chance gave a snort of disgust. ''Every dime went to pay off Mason Gabriel.''

Harlan's head came up sharply. ''Who?''

''Their father's partner.'' Ally smiled. ''Cody told me the whole story. How they pooled their money to get into a poker game in Monte Carlo, and ended up winning this land. When they saw what they'd won, Wes Wilde fell in love with the land, and decided to try his hand at ranching. But Mason Gabriel didn't want any part of it. All he wanted was his half, so he could go back to doing what he did best—gambling. Wes worked himself into an early grave struggling to pay off his partner and have enough left over to keep his family from starvation.''

Hazard nodded. ''Our lives would have been a whole lot easier if Mason Gabriel had stayed and worked this place with our dad. As it is, the four of us busted our...'' He paused and glanced at the women. ''...Busted our backs just to pay off that crazy coot. I've often wondered if he was smart enough to hold on to some of it for his old age, or gave it all away on the tables.''

Chance snorted. ''I'd lay odds he's lost it all. Dad never did consider him a very good gambler. The only reason he took him in as a partner was because he couldn't scrape up enough money to go it alone.''

Maggie carried a six-layer torte to the table and began slicing it. "While we're filling in bits and pieces of family history, how about some dessert?"

Erin poured coffee while Ally added a dollop of ice cream to each slice before passing them around. The three women worked in easy, companionable silence.

At a knock on the door they all looked up. A head covered with bright orange hair poked through the doorway, followed by a scratchy, tobacco-roughened voice. "Hello, Wilde bunch. How are my favorite cowboys?"

"Thelma." The three brothers were on their feet and crossing the room to greet the owner of the E.Z. Diner with warm hugs.

"You're just in time for dessert," Maggie called to her.

"Good. I see I haven't lost my touch. But I wish you wouldn't interrupt these men while they're kissing me. Go on, gentlemen. Show me again how happy you are to see me." With a throaty laugh Thelma offered her cheek for their kisses before greeting Cody and Erin.

Spying Harlan Brady seated across the table she stopped in her tracks. Something seemed to pass over her features. Something that softened all the lines and angles. It took her a moment before she could find her voice. "Harlan."

He was staring at her with a steady, unblinking gaze that was disquieting. At last he managed to say, "Thelma."

For a moment nobody spoke.

Finally Thelma said, "So. It's true then."

Chance glanced from one to the other. "What's true, Thel?"

She shook her head, sending the orange hair dancing.

"I came out here to see about a rumor that's been flying around Prosperous all day. I heard it said that Harlan Brady was staying at the Double W. I called them all a pack of liars. And now…" She glanced at Harlan again. "I find that I'm wrong. You're actually here."

"Not just me." He nodded toward Ally. "My granddaughter is here, too."

Thelma's eyes lit with pleasure. "This is little Allison?" She accepted her handshake and studied her. "You've grown into a beautiful young lady. You might not remember, but you used to come to my place with your grandfather."

"I remember." Ally's smile widened. "I remember that you always gave me an extra helping of whipped cream on those chocolate éclairs I loved."

"That's right. And you'd leave my place all sticky, and Harlan would tell me that his daughter-in-law would probably want to tan his hide." She shook her head. "He doted on you, honey."

"I know." Ally nodded. "The feelings were and are mutual."

"Come on, Thel." Maggie indicated a chair. "Have some coffee and some of my chocolate torte."

"Don't mind if I do." Thelma took a seat and studied the dessert. "You know, Maggie girl, this looks pretty enough to be on a magazine cover."

"Thanks. Now taste it and tell me if it's as good as it looks."

Thelma tasted, then closed her eyes. "Oh, I do miss your cooking. Sure you don't want to leave Chance and come back to work for me?"

"What would you do with your cook, Slocum?"

"He's off in jail again. I'm not sure I'm going to

bail him out this time. So how about it? I'll give you a raise.''

Maggie grinned at her husband. ''That's awfully tempting, Thel. But there are certain…perks in this job that you couldn't provide.''

''He's that good, huh?'' With a chuckle Thelma polished off her dessert, then sat back sipping coffee. ''Okay. Now tell me what's going on out here?''

''Not much.'' Chance topped off her cup. ''What's going on in Prosperous?''

''Don't play cool with me, boy.'' She gave a throaty laugh and turned to Harlan. ''All right. You tell me. What causes the man who vowed to never set foot on Wilde property to break his vow? Not only to break his vow, but to break bread with his enemy?''

Harlan started to look away, then lifted his chin and met her steady look with one of his own. ''It wasn't by choice.''

Thelma's eyes widened. ''What are you saying? They hog-tied you and forced you here against your will? Come on. Tell me what happened?''

When he didn't respond, Ace answered for him. ''Somebody shot his dog and set fire to his workroom in the barn. I brought him here so Hazard could treat his dog's injuries. And then we persuaded him and Ally to stay.''

Thelma pinned Harlan with a steady look. ''Did you see who did it?''

He nodded. ''A stranger. I've never seen him before. But there was real hatred in that man's eyes.''

''And a lie on his lips,'' Ace added. ''He told Harlan he was doing this on orders from the Wilde family.''

''Not again. After all these years.'' Thelma glanced from Ace to Harlan. ''Have you told them?''

The old man's eyes blazed. "You think they don't know?"

"I know they don't." She watched him for several long moments, then took a deep breath and set down her cup. "All right. I see it's up to me. Years ago, when your daddy first came here, he tried to buy Harlan's property."

Ace nodded. "We know that. And from what we've heard, he offered more than the fair market value."

"Which Harlan refused." Thelma glanced at him, then away. "Right after that, things started happening at Harlan's ranch."

"Things?" Ace leaned forward.

"Accidents. Some cattle found slaughtered. An outbuilding burned. Then the threats got personal. A caller threatened Harlan's family. That's when his son and daughter-in-law fled, taking little Allison with them."

Ally turned to her grandfather. "Why didn't you ever tell me?"

He said nothing.

Thelma glanced at those seated around the table. Her rough voice lowered. "The rumors flying around town were that Wes Wilde was determined to get Harlan's property, no matter what it took. There were a lot of folks willing to believe it."

"How about you, Thel?" Ace asked.

She placed a hand over his. "Ace, honey, I knew your daddy better'n most. It was Wes who gave me my first break in life. He not only persuaded old Oscar Stern to hire me, but when Oscar wanted to sell the restaurant and go live with his sister, it was your daddy who loaned me the money, even though he was struggling with his own debt. And he never asked a thing in return."

Harlan slapped a hand on the table, catching everyone by surprise. "You could have come to me for the money. You didn't have to go to Wes Wilde."

Thelma's tone was uncharacteristicly soft. "I know that's always been a sore spot between us, Harlan. You think I somehow betrayed you. But the truth is, I never went to Wes for help. He saw a need and came to me. That's the kind of man Wes Wilde was. He was good and honest and decent."

"I've heard enough." Harlan pressed the button, sending his scooter backing from the table. At the door to the kitchen he paused long enough to say, "I expect someone to take me home in the morning. I've had just about all the…sugarcoated testimonials honoring Saint Wes I can take."

When he was gone, an awkward silence settled over the room. From his vantage point, Ace thought he saw Thelma blink a tear from her eye before she busied herself with her coffee.

Cody shoved back his chair. "Thanks for dinner, Maggie."

"You're welcome, Cody."

The old cowboy walked to the back door and retrieved his hat. With his hand on the door he said, "For what it's worth, I heard those rumors, too. Never believed them then. Don't believe them now. And there's a lot more like me around."

He walked out, shutting the door softly behind him.

The three brothers fell silent for a moment.

It was Ace who finally said, "Is there anything else we haven't heard, Thelma?"

She shrugged. "Not much, I guess. I'm sorry I had to be the one to tell you this. You ought to know, a lot of folks who believed the rumors about your daddy did so because he was an outsider. A newcomer. They stood rock-solid behind Harlan because his family's been here for generations. But you boys have paid your dues. There's nobody in Prosperous who would believe such a rumor now.''

''I wouldn't be too sure of that.'' Chance closed a hand over his wife's. ''Somebody's going to a lot of trouble to plant a seed of suspicion, not only in Harlan's mind, but in the minds of everyone else as well. What I want to know is who and why? Who would benefit from ruining our reputation? What could he possibly hope to achieve?''

Thelma shook her head. ''I wish I knew. I didn't understand it when it was happening to your daddy, and I don't understand it today.''

''But there has to be a connection.'' Ace's tone was thoughtful. ''This isn't just a coincidence.''

While the others finished their dinner, and bid Thelma good-night, he remained lost in his own dark thoughts. A man like Wes Wilde was bound to have made some enemies. The key was to find out who they were, and then systematically check each one out. This wasn't some ghost from the past. This was a flesh-and-blood person out for revenge. And Ace had no intention of relaxing his guard until the man was found and stopped. This time for good.

''Did Thelma ever come out to your grandfather's ranch?'' Ace lay with his arms around Ally, his lips pressed to her temple. After the others had retired for the night, he'd made his way to her room, where they had come together in a storm of passion. Now they lay satisfied, content.

''Not that I recall.'' Ally curled herself close, loving

the feel of those strong arms around her. "But we spent a lot of time at her diner. My mother used to complain about the fact that Gramps hauled me along with him on that long drive into town almost every day."

"Maybe he was using you for a cover."

"Cover?"

"Yeah. Pretending that he was only there because you loved her chocolate éclairs."

"I did."

"Which gave him the perfect excuse to see her often."

"You think there was something between my grandfather and…?" She stopped to consider the implications.

"Did you notice how mad he got when she talked about accepting help from my father?"

"Jealousy?" Ally sat up. "Even after all these years, you think Gramps is jealous of your father?"

"I can't think of a stronger reason to hold a grudge for a lifetime than the love of a woman."

"Oh, Ace." She sank back down and wrapped her arms around his waist, pressing her cheek to his chest. "I need time to think about this. He's my grandfather."

"Yeah. And a man who's been alone for a lot of years. Have you ever wondered why? Maybe he's still carrying a torch."

"Over Thelma?" The thought brought a smile to her lips. "You know, even when I was a kid, I could see past that awful hair and gravelly voice to the soft heart underneath."

"Yeah, that's our Thel. She's always been there for my brothers and me. Like Agnes, she's a bulldog about the people she cares about."

"My grandfather and Thelma Banks." Ally closed

her eyes, listening to the strong, steady heartbeat beneath her ear. "As strange as it seems, I think you may have hit on something. But why, if there was a spark between them, did they stay apart all these years?"

He shrugged. "Who knows? Maybe because she defended my father when everyone else was ready to condemn him. I guess, for a proud man like Harlan, nursing a deep and abiding hatred that he thought well-founded, that would be the last straw."

Ally drew herself up to stare into Ace's eyes. "If it's true, think how sad it is. Two old people who could have spent these past years together have been apart and aching with loneliness. And all because of some cruel hoax being played by some...some madman."

"That's what worries me the most about all this." Ace's eyes darkened with feeling. "Whoever is doing this has to be filled with a sort of madness. Anger that would last this long would have to be fueled by more than petty jealousy or a careless misunderstanding. We're dealing with someone who's crossed the line."

He drew her into a fierce embrace and pressed his lips to a tangle of hair at her temple. "Promise me you'll try to keep your grandfather here tomorrow. No matter how desperately he wants to return home. We need just a little more time."

"I'll try, Ace."

"That's my girl." He brushed butterfly kisses over her forehead, her cheeks, her mouth. "And promise me you won't be alone at his ranch. Not even for an hour."

"All right. I'll see that I'm never alone." She traced the frown line that had formed between his brows. "Now stop worrying and kiss me, cowboy."

He did. Then on a sigh he took the kiss deeper.

Against her mouth he muttered, "Have you noticed how well I'm learning to take orders?"

"I have. And I'm proud of you. Now, if you wouldn't mind, I'd like you to..."

Her words were abruptly cut off as he anticipated her request and took her on a long, slow journey of love.

But later, as she slept in his arms, the frown was back. As was the nagging fear that he was overlooking something. Something so tantalizing close, like a whisper on the wind, he could almost grasp it, before it drifted just out of reach.

Chapter 14

"**Y**eah. The copter's already warming up." Ace spoke into the phone while the others were gathered around the breakfast table. "I should be up at the mine within the hour."

He hung up and drained a cup of coffee before snatching up his briefcase. "Thanks, Maggie. Got to run."

As always, Ally found herself wishing she could go along. She loved being with Ace. And she had enjoyed her employment, however brief, at the mine.

She walked with him to the porch. "I'll miss you."

He kissed her hard and quick. "Not as much as I'll miss you." He held her a little away. "You'll keep your grandfather here?"

"If I have to rope and hog-tie him."

"Good. I'll see you tonight." He kissed her again, then made a dash toward the waiting helicopter.

As Ally walked inside, Harlan was saying to Cody,

"Think you could spare enough time to drive me back to my place this morning?"

Behind Harlan's back she shook her head.

The old cowboy shrugged. "I'll have to see what chores Hazard wants me to see to first. He's the one who gives the orders here at the Double W. But if he gives the word, I'd be happy to drive you."

Harlan turned his scooter away from the table. "Then I guess I'd better go find your boss."

He made his way toward the lab, with Ally trailing behind. In the doorway he paused. Hazard looked up from the intravenous pack he was preparing.

"How's my old dog doing?" Harlan demanded.

"He's amazing. Just keeps improving every day." Hazard turned his back to insert a new IV in the old dog's leg.

"I was hoping to take him home today."

Hazard adjusted the tube, then ruffled the dog's head before getting to his feet. "I'm sorry. I know you're in a hurry to leave. But I think Buster needs one more day."

"You're sure? I'd take really good care of him back at my place."

"I know you would, Harlan." Hazard glanced beyond the old man to where Ally stood watching and listening. "But I'm going to have to insist that my patient remain here at least another day."

At Harlan's grudging nod of assent, Ally slowly released the breath she'd been holding. She'd feared she would have to engage in a shouting match to keep her grandfather here. But Hazard had managed it with a few simple words. As her grandfather rolled closer to the cage, where the two dogs lay side by side, Ally caught sight of the grin on Hazard's lips. And realized

that Ace had left nothing to chance. He'd already taken
his brother into his confidence.

"Well." She turned away with a smile. "I guess I'll
go help Maggie in the kitchen."

Minutes later, when the call came from the insurance
agent, her spirits lifted even more. "Yes. Of course I
can meet the appraiser at my grandfather's place." She
went in search of a vehicle. This day was just getting
better and better.

"Ace, we've got that first shipment ready to go."
The mine foreman's voice crackled over the speakerphone.

"Thanks, Kent. We're running ahead of schedule."

"Yep. Thought you'd want to know."

Ace rang off, then looked up as one of the staff from
the legal department stepped into his office and handed
him a thick folder.

"This is the Boyd contract you requested."

He nodded.

"Mr. Boyd wants confirmation by noon."

"He'll have it."

Before Ace could read the first line, the phone rang.
He absently picked up the receiver. "Ace Wilde."

"Thorpe here. As we'd hoped, Marla Craine has
made her move. She phoned a number in Prosperous."

"Is this the man who paid her?"

"Yes. We weren't certain at first. But now we're
sure of it."

Ace tensed. The file in his hand was forgotten.

"Who is it?"

"The man's name is Martin Gardner."

Ace shook his head. "It doesn't ring any bells."

"That's because it's turned out to be an alias. It took

my operatives a while to learn his true identity. He's a man who moves around a lot, and has no permanent address. But he's lived at a number of different locations in and around Las Vegas. His real name is Mason Gabriel.''

"Gabriel." For the space of a heartbeat Ace was thunderstruck. ''My father's old partner.'' A few more pieces were beginning to fit. ''Great work, Thorpe. Contact the sheriff. Tell him where Gabriel is staying in Prosperous. Let him know that we intend to press charges. I figure, by the time you complete your investigation, we'll have a whole lot more on him than just attempted sabotage against WildeMining.''

"I'll phone the sheriff as soon as I hang up.''

Ace disconnected, then dialed the ranch. ''Hazard? Thorpe just gave me the name of the man who paid my employee to sabotage our government deal. It was Dad's old partner, Mason Gabriel.''

He heard his brother's quick intake of breath. ''Gabriel?''

"Yeah. He's staying in town under an alias. I told Thorpe to alert the sheriff and have him picked up.''

"The bastard.'' Hazard's tone hardened. ''What do you think this is all about?''

"I don't know.'' Ace took a deep breath. ''But I figure between Thorpe and the sheriff, they'll get to the bottom of it all. Now, did our plan work? Is Harlan still there?''

Hazard chuckled. ''Worked like a charm. Just like you said. The old man's dying to get away from us, but not at the expense of that old dog's health. So I just told him Buster needed one more day.''

"Great.'' Ace joined in the laughter. He could feel

the tension slowly draining away. "Let me talk to Ally."

"She's not here, Ace. She borrowed one of our trucks. She's meeting the insurance adjuster over at her grandfather's ranch. He wants to appraise the damage and issue a check so they can get started rebuilding."

Ace sat up straighter. "I told her not to go there. Why didn't you send Cody or one of the wranglers along?"

"She won't be alone, Ace. She's meeting the adjuster. She wrote his name here somewhere." Ace could hear the shuffling of papers on the other end of the phone. "Yeah. Here it is. Martin Gardner."

Ace closed his eyes against a wave of shock. When he could find his voice he said, "Get hold of the sheriff. Tell him Mason Gabriel isn't in Prosperous. He's out at Harlan's ranch. And he has Ally."

Ally parked the Double W truck beside the shiny sedan. As she strode toward the house she felt a quick tug at her heart. She'd always loved this place so. It just cheered her to know that Gramps would soon be back in his workroom, doing the work that gave him so much pleasure.

She knew these past few days had been hard on him. But soon, she told herself, he would be back on his own land. Doing the work that he loved.

"Mr. Gardner?" She stepped into the burned-out shell of the barn and peered around in the gloom.

On the far side of the building she could make out a man, standing in the shadows.

"I'm so glad your company decided to handle this promptly. You'll never know what it means to my grandfather and me to get started on rebuilding."

He stayed where he was, allowing her to pick her way through the ashes and debris. When she reached him, she offered her hand. "Mr. Gardner? I'm Allison Brady."

He took her hand and smiled. But when she started to withdraw her hand, he grasped it firmly, holding her when she tried to pull away. At first she was merely puzzled. But when she looked up into his eyes, she felt a sudden surge of fear. His smile was gone. In its place was a look of pure hatred.

She yanked her hand free and started to back away. He reached out to a spot against some fallen timbers. When he straightened he was holding a rifle.

Ally's eyes rounded with fear. "Who are you?"

"An old friend of the family, my dear. Come to collect a debt."

Despite the gun in his hands she turned and started to run. She steeled herself, waiting for the report of gunfire. When it didn't come, she chanced a quick look over her shoulder. He was close on her heels.

She cleared the burned-out barn and was halfway to the house when she felt his hand close over her shoulder. She managed to wrench free, but it caused her to stumble. As she pitched forward, his big hands closed around her throat and began to squeeze.

She fought desperately, kicking, biting. But nothing would dislodge those hands, cutting off her breath until spots danced in front of her eyes, and she lost consciousness.

Ace drove by sheer instinct, negotiating the rutted road without really seeing it. Dust rose up around the vehicle as he pushed it to the limit, careening around twists and turns. He glanced at the fuel gauge, hoping the mine truck he'd commandeered didn't have an empty tank.

In his whole life he'd never known fear. It was an alien emotion to a reckless gambler who'd lived his whole life on the edge. But he tasted it now. A bitter, metallic burning in his throat as he thought about Ally in the clutches of a madman.

As the ranch came into view, his fear grew when he caught sight of a Double W truck parked beside a plain black sedan.

He came to a screeching halt beside the other vehicles and slammed out of the truck. A man stood on the porch, holding a rifle. Before Ace managed two steps, a gunshot rang out, spewing dust at his feet.

"Hold it right there, Wilde."

"What have you done with Ally?"

"You mean Allison Brady? She's in here. All cozy and comfortable. Want to see?" The man waved the rifle. "Just keep your hands where I can see them."

As Ace started forward the man reached into his pocket and removed something small and shiny.

"What's that?" Ace squinted against the sunlight.

"Another weapon." The man laughed at his joke. "Just a little backup, to see that you don't try anything foolish."

When Ace reached the porch the man held the door and Ace stepped inside, then froze.

Ally was seated on one of the kitchen chairs, her hands and ankles bound with cord. All around her feet colorful rag rugs had been bunched and mounded. The smell of gasoline was almost overpowering. It lay in puddles and formed a small stream from the door to where Ally sat.

Ace realized at once what the other weapon was. A

lighter. One spark, and Ally would be engulfed in flame.

He swallowed, struggling to control his fury. "You okay, Red?"

At the sound of his voice, Ally felt her eyes fill. She'd been trying to be so brave. But seeing Ace, and hearing him call her Red, had a sob backing up in her throat.

She lifted her chin. "I'm fine."

Ace saw the bruises on her throat, and more on her upper arms, and knew that she'd put up a fight. He struggled to bank his anger and keep his voice calm. "Your fight isn't with her. It's with me. If you promise to let her go, I'll let you tie me in her place without a fight."

The man's brows lifted. "Oh, this is rich. I've caught myself a hero." His voice lowered. "Or is there more here than heroics? Have you fallen for Harlan Brady's granddaughter?"

He saw the look that passed between Ace and Ally, and threw back his head to roar with laughter. "Now this is even better than I'd planned."

"What did you plan, Gabriel? What is this all about?"

"You know me?" The man's eyes widened in surprise.

"I know that Martin Gardner is an alias, and that you're really Mason Gabriel, my father's old partner." He heard the gasp of surprise from Ally, and forced himself not to look at her. He couldn't bear to see the bruises that marred her skin. "What I don't know is why you're here."

"I'm here to get what's owed me."

"I don't understand. My father paid you off years ago."

"Yeah. That's right. Paid me off. He gave me a measly half million dollars, then left his sons a ranch worth a hundred times that much."

"He paid you a fair market value. That's what you demanded. If you'd stayed to work it, you could have had half of everything."

"Yeah, well I had other fish to fry." His smile returned. "I lived like a king in Vegas. Mr. G. That's what they called me. What'll it be, Mr. G? What would you like, Mr. G? The penthouse suite? It's yours, Mr. G. A high-rollers game tonight, Mr. G? A couple of ladies to entertain you, Mr. G?" His smile faltered. "Then I got on a losing streak. I phoned your dad and told him I needed money. He said he'd paid all he owed me. So I asked him about this miserable piece of land. I knew it always stuck in his craw that he couldn't buy it. But if old Harlan could be persuaded to part with it, I figured your old man would owe me half. So I flew out here and decided to 'persuade' the old man to let it go."

Ace's eyes narrowed. For the first time, it was all beginning to make sense. "You were the one who threatened Harlan Brady?"

"Yeah. I hung around town and kept my ear to the ground, picking up any little bits of gossip I could. I learned that Harlan Brady's son and daughter-in-law wanted out of ranching. Figured the old man would be willing to take the money and run. When that didn't work, I decided to scare him off."

"You don't know my grandfather." Ally's eyes blazed.

"Oh, but I do. I made it a point to learn all I could

about him. And I found his soft spot. His only weakness.'' Gabriel pinned Ally with a look. "You. I've been waiting for you to come back. And when you finally did, I decided to make my move. You see, my plans are a lot grander than they used to be. Before, I just wanted half. Now I want all.''

Ace studied the man who stood with a rifle in one hand, a lighter in the other. In his eyes was a look of madness. That made him a whole lot more than just dangerous. It made him a deadly opponent. The burned-out shell of the barn just beyond the windows was a jolting reminder that Mason Gabriel didn't bluff. He played for keeps.

"All right, Gabriel. I'll ask you again. Let me change places with Ally. This fight is really about us. It has nothing to do with her.''

"That's the beauty of all this. Don't you see? When her body is found, the town will rise up against the Wilde brothers. There isn't a jury in this state that won't believe you finally took the revenge your father sought all those years ago. And when the trial is over, I'll come forward with a deed to the property.''

"What deed?''

Gabriel gave a sly smile. "Let's just say I have friends in low places. They can get me any document, for a price. A document that will stand up in any court in this land. And with the Wilde brothers out of the way, I'll sell off old Wes Wilde's empire and go back to living like a king.''

Ace glanced around for something, anything, to use as a weapon. He would have but one chance to take this madman out. Otherwise, a single spark from his lighter would end everything. "It sounds like you've been planning this for a long time, Gabriel.''

Mason Gabriel gave a chilling laugh. "Who do you think paid off Iris Arnold at WildeOil to doctor that multimillion dollar contract a few months ago? All I had to do was remind her that it was Chance Wilde who had caused her father to leave his wife and children, when he'd feared being fired."

"That was a lie and you know it."

"But Iris didn't know that." He sneered. "And who do you think fed the flames of hatred in Russ Thurman, and got him to take out his anger on your brother Hazard's cattle?"

For the space of a full minute Ace couldn't believe what he'd heard. His voice deepened with fury. "You caused all those problems? The investigation of all the employees at WildeOil? The loss of all those cattle at the Double W?"

"That's me. The little fly in your ointment, Wilde. Flitting here, flitting there, planting a rumor here, a lie there. Before long, there are all kinds of old enemies waiting to take potshots at the Wilde brothers. But since none of them succeeded in taking you out entirely, I realized it was up to me to step in and do the job myself." He flicked open the lighter and a tiny, deadly flame danced in his hand. "And now this fly is going to flit outside. Wouldn't want to get too close to the explosion that's about to take place." He laughed. "Let's see if you can untie your ladylove in time to save her."

"No!" Ace leapt across the space that separated them. But even as he did, he knew it was too late.

As he hurtled through the air, gunfire roared, and pain exploded through his upper body. Through sheer determination he kept on going. His hands clutched at Gabriel's shirtfront. He heard the fabric tear as he struggled to make contact with slippery flesh. He saw the lighter arc like a flaming torch and land in a puddle of liquid, just as Gabriel disappeared through the doorway. And then all he could see was a thin line of fire streaking toward the gasoline-soaked rugs at Ally's feet.

Raw panic scraped over his nerves as he struggled to outrace the flame. But the bullet to his shoulder had left him sluggish. By the time he was struggling with the cords that bound her hands and ankles, there was a wall of fire around them, scorching their hair, searing their flesh, burning every breath they dragged into their oxygen-starved lungs.

"Hang on, Red." Ace's fingers felt stiff and awkward as he fumbled with her bonds. He discovered to his horror that she was not only bound at the hands and feet, but tied to the chair as well.

By now their clothes were smoldering, and the heat so intense, they could no longer breathe. In desperation he lifted her, chair and all, and raced through the leaping flames and billowing smoke to freedom just beyond the door.

For several seconds they lay in the dirt, choking and coughing as they dragged air into their lungs. Seeing smoke curling from Ally's clothes, and from the legs of the chair, Ace smothered it with his body. Then, panting from the effort, he lifted his head.

"Are you all right, Red?"

She nodded, too overcome to reply. The front of his shirt was stained with his blood. So much blood. She marveled that he could remain conscious. Still, she knew it was only a matter of moments before he would lose the battle to remain awake.

Smoke still curled from the cord binding her hands

and ankles, and she realized it had burned clear through. It seemed too much effort to even lift herself free. But she managed to squeeze Ace's hand.

He glanced down and saw that she was no longer bound. He started to draw her toward him, then froze.

"You must have some kind of luck, Wilde, to come through all that alive."

At the ominous tone, Ace looked up to see Mason Gabriel standing over him. In his hands was the rifle. Pointed directly at Ace's head.

"But I'm about to end your lucky streak right now."

"How are you going to explain the gunshot?" Every word Ace spoke strained his raw lungs.

"I'll tell the authorities you tried to burn down the Brady ranch, with his granddaughter inside. I had no choice but to save her and shoot you." Mason touched a hand to his heart in mock sadness. "Unfortunately, the little lady was overcome by smoke, and expired." He grinned. "Even an autopsy won't prove otherwise. Her lungs are full of smoke. A plastic bag over her head will just end it." He threw back his head and laughed. A high, thin sound of dementia that scraped over their already ragged nerves. "I'll probably be hailed as a hero for ridding Wyoming of such a dastardly villain."

Ace felt a wave of despair. Not for himself. His life no longer mattered. But the thought of Ally's fate had him nearly crazed with determination. He had to do something now, before he lapsed into unconsciousness.

Calling on every ounce of energy, he got to his feet and took several halting steps to one side, hoping to keep Gabriel's attention focused away from Ally. He prayed she'd have the sense to run while he kept the gunman distracted.

"What happens if her grandfather refuses to sell to you?"

"He'll have a little…accident. Who'd question an old cripple falling off his scooter and left exposed to the elements for a couple of nights?"

Out of the corner of his eye Ace saw Ally roll free of the chair. His hopes began to rise. Now, if she could make it as far as his truck, she would find the keys still in the ignition.

"You've thought of everything, haven't you, Gabriel?"

"I've had a lot of years to plan my revenge against you and your brothers. Especially after your old man cheated me out of hurting him."

"I don't understand what you mean."

"I spent years plotting and scheming how to hurt Wes Wilde. I was having such a good time causing all those little…accidents on this ranch, and then watching Wes take the blame. But then I made the mistake of phoning him, and telling him what I was doing. Oh, I enjoyed myself immensely when he lost his temper and threatened to go to the authorities. I reminded him that nobody would believe such a crazy story. I knew that got to him. But then I guess it was all too much for him. I heard he keeled over in the barn and died of a heart attack that same day. I never forgave your father for dying before the fun was over."

From her vantage point on the ground, Ally struggled frantically to stand, but found, to her despair, that her legs wouldn't support her. She looked around, desperate to save Ace from this madman. Her heart was pounding in her chest when she caught sight of the look of absolute disbelief on his face when he heard what Mason Gabriel had just said.

Ace's voice was choked. His vision clouded by a red mist of fury. "You caused my father's heart attack?"

Mason gave a wide smile. "Oh, this is so good. Do you know, when you're in a temper like you are now, you look just like him? So, if I can't have the satisfaction of killing Wes Wilde, at least I'll kill his lookalike son."

Ace's crippling pain was forgotten. Everything was forgotten except the rage that drove him. He started forward, unmindful of the rifle pointed at his head. "You're a dead man, Gabriel."

Ace saw Gabriel's finger tighten on the trigger. But before he could squeeze off a shot, he suddenly screamed and clutched both hands to his face. The rifle fell to the ground.

Ace looked over and saw Ally kneeling in the dirt, holding two broken chair legs like pool sticks. The rock she'd fired in place of a cue ball had scored a direct hit in Gabriel's eye with all the force of a missile.

It was all the advantage Ace needed. With a string of oaths he landed a blow that had Mason reeling backward. Then Ace began pummeling him with his fists, landing blow after blow to his head and face. Mason dropped to his knees and Ace stood over him, waiting to hit him again. Instead Gabriel brought his head up with such force it sent Ace sprawling backward. Before he could recover Gabriel began kicking him in the face and body, unleashing a brutal assault until he was a mass of bloodied flesh.

Amazingly, Ace struggled to his feet one more time, but the bullet had taken its toll. He found he couldn't will his arm to move.

Mason reared back and hit him with all his strength, sending him sprawling in the dirt.

"Stop it." Ally wasn't even aware of the tears that streamed from her eyes, nearly blinding her. All she knew was that she had to stop this madman before he killed Ace.

"Shut up. I'll deal with you when I've finished with him." Gabriel stooped down to grab the rifle.

But Ally was there first. Fear had given her renewed strength. She snatched it up, then took a step back, aiming it at his chest. "Move away from Ace, or I'll fire."

Gabriel paused for only a moment. Seeing the fear in her eyes, and the way her hands trembled, he began to laugh. "All my life I've been a gambling man. And right now, I'm about to take the biggest gamble of my life. I'm calling your bluff. I don't believe you have the guts to pull that trigger."

"Don't," she cried. She glanced at Ace, then back at Gabriel, and realized he had no intention of stopping his torment.

As he reached for her, there was a thunderous explosion. For a moment the man facing her paused, staring at her in mute surprise. Then, as he clutched at his chest, a river of blood spilled through his hands, staining the front of his shirt and pooling on the ground at his feet. He went rigid, before dropping to his knees and falling forward in the dirt.

"Ace." Ally rushed to his side, kneeling beside him, tears rolling down her face. "Oh, Ace. Please don't die."

"...Not dead." He managed the words over a bloody, swollen mouth.

"Thank God. You're alive. But...I've shot Mason Gabriel. I may have killed him." The tears came harder and faster now.

"Shhh." Against a wave of pain he struggled to sit up, and nearly passed out cold. "Do you realize...just saved both our lives?"

"But I've... Oh, Ace. I pulled the trigger."

"Come here, Red."

Sobbing, she fell into his arms, needing to touch his face, to feel his strength, to assure herself that he was, indeed, alive.

As for Ace, he'd never known his heart to beat so erratically. As though he'd been swimming through quicksand. But now, someone had tossed him a lifeline. He closed his eyes and held on, allowing himself to drift on the peaceful current. And vowed that even when he reached shore, he was never, ever again, going to let go.

Chapter 15

"All these years. All this hatred and jealousy. And it was all over money." Chance shook his head, as Ace recounted everything Mason had told him.

They were in the great room. Ace lay on the sofa, swathed in bandages after an airlift to the hospital in Laramie. Ally had never left his side. She sat now, holding his hand, listening quietly as he fielded their questions.

"What happens to a man, that he can get so caught up in revenge?" Erin asked softly.

"I don't know." Hazard shook his head. "Seems like such a waste of a life. If he had put half that energy into pursuing something positive, he could have been wealthy and successful in his own right."

"Huh." Agnes huffed into the room and pressed a hand to Ace's forehead. Satisfied, she nodded. "I'm just glad you were able to stop the madness."

"It wasn't my doing." Ace smiled at Ally. "Here's the real heroine of the day. If she hadn't reacted when she did, we'd both be dead now."

For a minute Agnes merely stared at Ally without words. Then, her lips trembling, she burst into tears before waddling out of the room.

The others fell silent. Ace glanced at Cody, who simply winked before staring down at his hands.

When Ally found her voice she wiped away a tear of her own. "How could I do less than you, Ace?" She turned to the others. "Even though he'd been shot, Ace managed to carry me, chair and all, through a wall of flame, and out of that inferno."

Harlan, who had been listening in stunned silence, cleared his throat. "And for that, I owe you, son."

Ace turned to him. "I'm just sorry that you had to lose everything. I hope you're insured."

"You saved the most important thing in my life. My granddaughter." The old man sighed. "As for the house and barn, I think there's enough to rebuild. But if you don't mind, it looks like my granddaughter and I will be accepting your hospitality awhile longer."

"Mind?" Ace's smile was dazzling. "I'm getting used to having her...and you, of course, and Buster and Billy, around."

The others grinned.

Maggie stifled a yawn. "I don't know about the rest of you, but I'm exhausted just thinking about all that went on today."

Chance stood and dropped an arm around his wife's shoulders. "That makes two of us."

As they walked away, Harlan brought his scooter closer and offered a hand to Ace. "Thanks, son, for being there for my granddaughter. I'm ashamed of all the years I've held a grudge against your family."

Solemnly the two men shook hands.

Harlan turned to Ally. "Good night, Allycat."

"'Night, Gramps." She wrapped her arms around his neck and hugged him fiercely. "I love you."

"And I love you. I don't know what I'd do if I ever lost you."

When he was gone she helped Ace to his feet. "Think you can make it to the bedroom?"

He shook his head. "Mine's too far away. I think I'd better stop at yours."

Behind him, Hazard and Erin laughed.

"Same old Ace," Hazard muttered against her ear.

"Uh-huh. I was thinking the same thing. Some things never change."

If Ace heard them, he never let on as he allowed Ally to help him into her room. When the door closed, he leaned against it and drew her into his arms.

"Are you okay?" she whispered.

"Oh, yeah. Better than okay. Red, I'm so glad to be standing here right now, just holding you. There were a few moments there when I was afraid I'd never have the opportunity to do this again."

And then, as his mouth covered hers, he listened to the sound of their beating hearts, and realized just what a gift they'd been given.

Ace lay in bed, his hands under his head, enjoying the familiar rituals of morning at the Double W. The air was spiced with cinnamon and apple, and he knew Maggie was baking one of her fabulous coffee cakes for breakfast. Somewhere a door slammed, and the sound of Chance shouting something to Hazard had him grinning.

Just outside his window, Buster and Billy were barking at the arrival of a truck. He heard the engine idle for a moment, then go quiet. The crunch of footsteps grew closer, and the back door was thrown open as Cody entered, calling a greeting.

The bedroom door opened and Ally stepped in looking all fresh and glowing from her shower. Behind her Buster and Billy padded to the bed. Billy leapt up and licked Ace's face, while Buster, still nursing his wound, had to be content to wait on the floor, his whole body wiggling with happiness.

Ally dressed quickly, in a shirt tied at the midriff and a pair of cotton shorts that showed off those long legs to their best advantage. Ace scratched Billy's ears and enjoyed the view.

"Coming to breakfast?" she called over her shoulder.

"Yeah. In a few minutes. You going to give me a kiss?"

She crossed to the bed and brushed her lips over his. He felt the slow simmer begin deep inside. Would it always be like this? he wondered. Would he never tire of the taste of her, the feel of her in his arms?

"Come on, Billy." She picked up the dog and started toward the door, with Buster lumbering behind.

"Where are you going?"

"To join the others. Coming?"

"Yeah." He swung his feet to the floor. "Soon as I shower. Tell Maggie to save me a piece of that coffee cake."

Ally grinned. But when she pulled the door closed,

her smile faded and she took a deep breath. This was going to be a lot harder than she'd thought. Every time she even looked at Ace, her heart did a series of somersaults, and her brain turned to mush.

She stiffened her shoulders and lifted her chin. She could do this. A little bit of fear couldn't stop her. After all, wasn't she the greatest hustler in the world?

She greeted the others and helped herself to a glass of juice. Agnes, who was just pouring herself a cup of coffee, poured one for Ally and handed it to her.

"Thanks, Agnes."

"You're welcome." The old woman cleared her throat. "You really going to go through with it?"

Ally nodded.

Agnes put a hand over hers and lowered her voice. "You and Ace belong together."

Ally felt her eyes fill and blinked furiously. "Thanks, Agnes. That's really sweet of you, but..."

"No buts. I've seen a lot of females making big eyes at that boy. But none of them were right. Now you...you're right."

She waddled away before Ally could argue.

The others got suddenly busy, pretending they hadn't overheard. Even Harlan, usually so outspoken, seemed subdued this morning. But all of them had privately agreed that Ace, no matter the assault on his heart, was a confirmed bachelor.

By the time Ace walked into the kitchen, they were gathered around the table enjoying breakfast.

"'Morning, all." Ace turned to Maggie. "Did you save me a piece of that coffee cake?"

"You know I wouldn't forget." She placed it in front of him and watched as he dug in.

He tasted, sighed, then finished the entire piece before reaching for the platter of eggs. As he did his glance fell on the suitcases by the door.

"Who's leaving?"

Ally turned to him with a smile. "I can see that Agnes was right. This last week of pampering seems to have affected your mind. I told you the insurance company is providing Gramps with a mobile home while the house and barn are being rebuilt."

"Yeah. I remember. So those are yours, Harlan? Why so many?"

"Half are mine," the old man said. "The other half belong to Allycat."

"You're…" He swiveled his head. "…Leaving, too?"

"You don't think I'd let Gramps go back there alone?"

"Yeah. I thought…" He looked around the table and realized that everyone was watching and listening. "Look. Could we go someplace alone and talk?"

"Talk?" Ally lowered her cup of coffee. "What's there to talk about, Ace?"

"About us. I thought, since we get along so well together, that you might…that we might…" He set down his knife and fork with a clatter. "This isn't easy for me to say. But I thought we might stay together."

"We can get together, Ace." She began gathering up her dishes before getting to her feet. As she crossed to the sink she said, "Now that you and Gramps are such good friends, you can come visit whenever you want. Even Buster and Billy will be happy to see you."

"That isn't what I meant." Annoyed, he tossed down his napkin.

"All right. Then I'll come here to visit, too. Often, if you'd like." She started rinsing the dishes, then placing them in the dishwasher.

Around the table, the others ate in silence.

"I want more." He shoved back his chair and stood facing her. "I was thinking maybe we'd...get married."

"Married?" Ally looked up, then shook her head. "You know you don't really want to get married, Ace. You're just saying that because you think it's what a woman wants to hear."

"Well? Don't you?" He could feel his temper rising. "After all, it isn't like I make this kind of offer every day of my life. In fact, damn it, you're the first woman I've ever said this to. I should think you'd give it a little more consideration than this."

"Oh. You want consideration?" She paused, stared at the ceiling, then smiled sweetly. "Okay. I've considered your proposal, Ace. But I'm afraid I'll have to decline."

"You can't mean this." He stalked closer, his hands balled into fists at his sides. "You love me. And I love you. Why shouldn't we get married?"

She shrugged, then to add insult to injury, patted his arm. "Because I like things the way they are. No strings. No commitments. We'll still get together. Have a few laughs."

"Laughs?" His eyes narrowed. "Is that what you think life is all about? A few laughs? A roll in the hay?"

"Ace." She straightened. Dried her hands. "Why should we spoil things? We're both feeling so good now. Let's not rock the boat."

"Whose boat? Yours or mine?"

"I thought we were both happy with the way things are. Aren't you happy, Ace?"

"No. Yes." He hissed out a breath. "Listen. I am happy. But I want it all, Red. I want marriage. Commitment. A family." He paused. "Is that it? Are you afraid to think about having a baby?"

She shrugged. "I haven't given it a lot of thought. But I suppose, when the time comes, I'll get used to the idea."

"Get used to…" He huffed out another breath. "Okay, look. I know it's different with you, Red. You had all those years to take care of your mother. And now you're worried about your grandfather. A husband and kids would just be more work for you. But I give you my word. If you agree to marry me, I'll share everything. I'll never ask you to take on more work than you really want."

She was shaking her head. "Ace, I don't think…"

"Wait." He caught her by the shoulders, and for a moment thought about shaking some sense into her. Then he seemed to catch himself. His touch gentled and he ran his hands up and down her arms. His tone turned persuasive. "Tell you what, Red. You agree to marry me, I'll do something I swore I'd never do."

"What's that?"

"I'll…go for the big wedding. You know. Tuxedo, flowers, the whole town of Prosperous invited. Hell, I'll even invite the whole state of Wyoming."

She shook her head.

"And I'll…" He started talking faster. "I'll live with you and your grandfather." At her look of surprise he nodded emphatically. "Really. It's closer to the mine anyway. While the builders are there, we'll have them build whatever kind of house you've always dreamed of having. And I'll…'' He dragged in a breath. He was on a roll now. ''I'll get Maggie's recipe for coffee cake. I'll get up early and bake it while you sleep in late.''

She pulled away and faced him, her hands on her hips. ''Now I know you're not being serious, Ace. You're just saying whatever you think I want to hear. When are you going to take no for an answer? Because that's my answer, Ace. Read my lips.''

Ace stormed over to the back door and turned the lock. Then, with everyone watching, he dropped the key in his pocket and leaned against the door. ''Okay, Red. Here's the deal. I have no intention of settling for an occasional visit. A few laughs. A few tumbles. You're not leaving the Double W until you agree to marry me. It's marriage or nothing.''

Like spectators at a tennis match, everyone at the table turned from Ace to Ally.

She stood across the room, her hands on her hips, staring at him as if she couldn't believe what she'd just heard.

''That's my only choice? Marriage or nothing?''

Ace took a deep breath, knowing he'd just backed himself into a corner. If she left him now, his future would be ashes. And his heart would be shattered beyond repair. ''That's right.''

She walked slowly toward him, her eyes on his. When she was close enough to touch him, she reached out a hand to his chest. ''Your pulse is a little overactive.''

''So's my imagination. What's your answer?''

She smiled, and he thought it was the most beautiful thing he'd ever seen. Batting her lashes, she looked up at him and said, "I'm just not strong enough to fight you, Ace. You know I couldn't bear to never see you again. So, since you leave me no other choice, I guess I'll marry you."

He gathered her close and pressed his lips to her temple. "I'm sorry about the strong-arm tactics, Red. But I was desperate. My life wouldn't be worth living without you. And I promise you, you'll never be sorry. I'll spend the rest of my life making you glad you married me."

She sighed and closed her arms around his waist, pressing her lips to his throat. Feeling extremely smug, he glanced over her head, and caught sight of the others. They were all smiling. And his two brothers were exchanging money.

Then he saw Cody grinning at him like a fool and the realization of what had just happened hit him with all the force of a thunderbolt. The man who had once boasted that no female would ever get him to propose had just made a promise of marriage.

He caught Ally by the shoulders and held her a little away. "Have I just been...hustled again?"

Her eyes widened. "You think the great pool hustler Ace Wilde has just been conned by little old me a second time?"

For the space of a full minute he merely stared at her. Then he threw back his head and roared, and the others joined in, until they were weak with laughter.

Harlan shook his head. "You have to admit, son. My Allycat may just be the best con artist in the world."

"It takes one to know one." Ace pressed his forehead to hers. "Do you realize, Red, if we ever have kids, they'll probably be the most successful little hustlers in the world?"

"I wouldn't be at all surprised." She brushed her lips over his and felt the quick rush of heat. Then she wrapped her arms around his neck. "Oh, Ace. I was so afraid you'd let me go without a fight."

"Not on your life, Red. You're too dangerous to have anywhere but right here beside me." He started to kiss her, and noticed out of the corner of his eye that Agnes was wiping away a tear and the others were watching with avid interest.

He lifted her in his arms and strode across the room. "Now if the rest of you don't mind, Ally and I have a few things to say to each other in private."

As the door closed behind them, Chance turned to Hazard. "Ten dollars says they don't come out for at least an hour."

Hazard shook his head. "I'm putting my money on noon."

They turned to Cody, who shook his head. "I'm out of this one. I think I'll drive Harlan over to his property. Maybe the two lovebirds will get there in time for dinner. If not, I'll bring him back here."

The two old men headed toward the door. Despite the fact that one had the lanky stride of a seasoned cowboy, and the other glided in a scooter, they wore identical smiles.

Harlan could be heard boasting, "That girl may be the best ever. Did I mention that I taught her everything she knows?"

Alone in their room, Ace drew Ally into the circle

of his arms and kissed her until they were both breathless. Then, as he reached for the buttons of her blouse, he kept his eyes steady on hers.

The voices and laughter in the other room had faded away. Now they were all alone. There was no need to speak. The love they felt was there in their eyes. In the gentleness of their touch. In the catch of their breath as they came together, as lovers have, from the beginning of time.

Epilogue

"Well, well, little bro. Don't you look pretty." Chance strolled into the library carrying a handful of crystal tumblers.

"I look like a damned penguin. But I promised Ally, so I'll see this thing through."

"You got that right." Hazard stood behind him, straightening his tie. "A deal is a deal."

Cody ambled in and paused in the doorway.

"What're you looking at?" Ace snarled.

"The three of you. This may be the last time I'll ever see you looking like headwaiters. Figured I'd better look while I can."

Ace grinned at his brothers. "He's right. We do look like waiters. Want to pass around trays of champagne to the crowd out there?"

Hazard glanced out the window. "You weren't exaggerating when you promised to invite all of Prosperous and the state of Wyoming. I think they all showed up.''

Chance nodded. ''Even the governor. But he's up for reelection. Probably figures he'll meet more people here than he will anyplace else.''

''I'm glad you talked Ally into having a barbecue supper after the wedding.'' Chance took an aged bottle of whiskey from a cabinet and began filling four tumblers. ''Maggie's in her glory out there. She's had the beef slow-roasting in the pits all night. And she's been up since dawn, instructing all those girls from town how to serve those fancy foods she's been dreaming up.''

He began passing out the tumblers. ''I'd like to make the first toast.'' He lifted his glass. ''Here's to Dad.''

They drank in silence.

''And here's to you, baby brother.'' Chance grinned. ''You gave me a lot of bad moments when you were growing up, but you've turned out just fine. I'm proud of you.''

''Thanks, bro. I'm proud of all three of us.''

They tossed back a second drink.

Hazard held up his glass. ''Here's to your bride. I think you've met your match with Ally. She's going to make you one damned fine wife.''

Ace grinned as they drank again.

Cody lifted his glass and cleared his throat. ''Ace. All I can say is, your daddy saved the best for last.''

Ace looked at the old cowboy, then drained his glass, wondering if the path of fire down his throat was from the whiskey or the lump he'd been forced to swallow.

He was relieved when a knock on the door broke the silence. Cody opened it to admit Maggie and Erin. Both women were beaming with excitement.

Ace turned to Chance. "When are you and Maggie moving?"

"Couple of weeks." Chance draped an arm around his wife's shoulders. "The house is almost ready."

"And it's a good thing," Maggie said with a smile. "We're soon going to be needing more room."

Before Ace could ask why, he saw Chance touch a hand to his wife's middle. He gaped. "A...baby?"

"That's right." Maggie was glowing.

"When?"

"By spring."

Ace kissed her cheek and pumped his brother's hand.

When everyone had offered their congratulations, Hazard looked at Ace. "I wish you and Ally would consider staying on at the Double W."

"Can't do it." Ace shook his head. "Ally needs to be close to her grandfather. They've been apart too long. Besides, it's much closer to the mine. It'll make my commute a lot easier."

Hazard gave a wry smile. "This old house is sure going to seem empty when you're all gone. Erin and I will be rattling around in here feeling lost."

Erin gave him a shy smile. "Then I think it's time we thought about filling this place with babies."

"You mean it?" Hazard was grinning from ear to ear.

"Why not?" She shrugged. "Why should Chance and Maggie have all the fun? Besides, wouldn't Agnes and Cody enjoy another generation of Wildes?"

"Oh, Erin." He kissed her, then looked at the others. "See why I love her?"

"Yeah." Ace set his tumbler aside and started toward the door.

"Were are you going?" Hazard called.

"All this talk about babies has me getting ideas. I want to see my bride-to-be. Right now."

Ace made his way along the hallway to the guest suite. The door was open. Inside, Harlan was seated in his scooter, facing Ally, whose back was to the door.

From his vantage point, Ace could see yards of white silk and lace, and masses of red hair that begged for his touch. For a moment he held back, enjoying the view. Then he could wait no longer. He stepped inside and crossed to her side.

"Ace." Her smile was radiant. "It's traditional for the groom to wait until the ceremony to see the bride."

"Red, there's nothing traditional about us." He brushed a kiss over her cheek. "Why start now?"

She laughed and turned to Harlan. "Are you sure you want me to go through with this, Gramps?"

"Absolutely." The old man looked as happy as his granddaughter. "I knew the first time I met him, he was the one for you."

"Yeah. Right. Until you found out my name," Ace said with a laugh.

"Well, that was a shock. But I'm getting over it."

"You'd better. We're going to be living awfully close to one another."

"I've been thinking about that." Harlan cleared his throat. "I'm pleased and proud that you two want to live on my little ranch, but after being here, with all this room, I'm worried that you'll start to feel confined."

"Harlan, if I had to live in one room, I'd be fine, as long as your granddaughter was in there with me."

The old man laughed. "Seeing the way you two look at each other, I'm inclined to believe you. But I want you to know that I intend to build my own workroom, with its own apartment. For whatever years I have left, I want to live my own life, doing exactly as I please.''

"That's all anybody wants." Ace reached into his pocket and handed Harlan a vial. "I brought you a gift.''

Harlan studied it with a puzzled frown. "Looks like dirt.''

"It is. From your ranch. I had some soil borings done.''

Harlan and Ally were both staring at him.

"You're a rich man, Harlan. Your ranch is sitting over one of the richest deposits of uranium in the state. Maybe in the country.''

Harlan's mouth opened, then closed. He couldn't seem to find his voice.

"From what I can see, Harlan, your fifty acres of hardscrabble land are as valuable as our one hundred fifty thousand acres here at the Double W. So you can build any kind of fancy workroom you please. You can hire assistants, if you want.''

"Why would I need assistants?''

Ace grinned. "Oh. Did I forget to mention? I bought you a computer, so you can start a website on the Internet. Within a few weeks you'll probably be getting orders for your saddles from people all over the world. You may have fallen off the face of the earth for a while, but you're back now. And ready to chase that old dream.''

"Oh, Gramps. Isn't this wonderful?" Ally fell into her grandfather's arms, and the two of them hugged each other fiercely.

When she stepped back, Harlan offered his hand-shake to Ace. "I don't know what to say. Or how to thank you.''

"Then don't." Ace gave him that famous Wilde grin. "I really did it so I'd be marrying an heiress."

At a knock on the door, they looked up to see Erin, beckoning. "Reverend Young is here. And the service is about to begin."

Harlan blew his granddaughter a kiss, then touched the button of his scooter and rolled from the room.

As Ally turned to follow him, Ace drew her back. "Wait a minute."

"Getting cold feet, cowboy?"

He laughed. "Not a chance. I had to fight too hard to get you to marry me."

"You forget. I was the one who hustled you."

"Were you?"

She turned and caught sight of that quick, dangerous grin. Her eyes narrowed. "Are you telling me you were pulling a con of your own?"

He drew her close and kissed the tip of her nose. "You'll never know, will you?"

"Oh, Ace." She managed a shaky laugh. "I never had a chance, did I?"

"No more than I did." He covered her mouth with his and allowed himself several long moments of pleasure.

They could hear the music starting in the other room, and the sound of voices growing hushed and expectant.

"I guess this is it, Red." He caught her hand. "I just thought I'd better warn you. Reverend Young is long-winded. And after his sermon, I've asked Agnes to say a few words."

"Agnes?"

He nodded. "She's losing her last boy, you know. She deserves to be part of this." He studied her eyes. "Do you mind?"

"Mind? Oh, Ace." She stood on tiptoe to brush her lips over his. "I think it's sweet. I guess I should have expected something like this from you."

"What does that mean?"

"You always do the unexpected."

He gave her a heart-stopping grin. "That's to keep you on your toes, Red."

With their fingers linked they made their way to the great room, crowded with guests. In front of a window banked with masses of flowers, Maggie and Chance stood to one side, with Erin and Hazard on the other. Between them stood the reverend, looking befuddled, and behind him Agnes Tallfeather, wearing a traditional Native American dress.

Ace and Ally had agreed that their wedding would be highly personalized. And so they walked in together, hands joined. The crowd held its breath at the handsome man and his stunning bride.

As they passed Harlan, they saw Thelma Banks seated beside him. The two were holding hands and looking relaxed and happy. Buster and Billy, wearing festive white collars entwined with flowers, sat on either side of them. When the two dogs caught sight of the bride and groom they started a chorus of happy barking that had everyone laughing.

Across the aisle, Cody sat beaming like a proud father.

As expected, Reverend Young gave one of his rambling sermons on the love of a man and woman. Through it all, Ace and Ally merely looked into each other's eyes and smiled. But when it came time to speak their vows, and exchange rings, their looks grew more serious. They forgot about everything except the moment.

And then, as they were pronounced husband and wife, Agnes walked forward.

In a soft voice that had everyone straining to hear she said, "Many years ago these words were spoken when I wed my husband, Louis. I share them with you, Ace, and you, Allison, because you are like my own." She placed her hands on their heads and said, "Now you will feel no rain, for each of you will be shelter to the other. Now you will feel no cold, for each of you will be warmth to the other. Now there is no loneliness, for each of you will be companion to the other." Her lips quivered as her hands lingered a moment on the head of this untamed, impulsive young man and his equally daring bride. "You are two persons, but now there is but one life between you. May your days be good and long upon this earth."

When she was finished, Ace rewarded her with a fierce bear hug.

"Oh, Agnes. Thank you." As Ally brushed a kiss over the old woman's cheek, she thought of all the years she had ever despaired of coming back to Wyoming. Of ever being reunited with her beloved grandfather. And now she would have it all. The chance to be with Gramps in his old age. The love of the man who owned her heart completely. This family, which made her feel so welcome, so complete. And best of all, this man. In Ace's arms, she truly had come home.

"Come here, Red." Ace drew her close, and in front of the assembled, kissed her soundly. Then, to much applause, he kissed her again until they were both laughing and breathless.

As the crowd surged forward to offer their congratulations, Ace extended his hand to his brothers. At the press of their hands over his, he felt a rush of gratitude to their father.

To others, Wes Wilde may have been a wild and reckless gambler who had risked all for a piece of wilderness which his sons had built into an empire. But his greatest legacy was right here in this room. Three sons who had stayed together despite enormous obstacles. Brothers who had chosen a path of honor, loyalty and love. And now this legacy of love would be passed on to a new generation. This, he suddenly realized, was the greatest gift of all.

* * * * *

*Don't miss delightful
author Ruth Langan's next
unforgettable miniseries,*

SIRENS OF THE SEA,

to debut in August 2000 with

THE SEA WITCH,

*available only from
Harlequin Historicals.*

presents a riveting 12-book continuity series:

A YEAR OF LOVING DANGEROUSLY

When dishonor threatens a top-secret agency, twelve of the best agents in the world are determined to uncover a deadly traitor in their midst. These brave men and women are prepared to risk it all as they put their lives—and their hearts—on the line. But will justice…and true love…prevail?

You won't want to miss a moment of the heart-pounding adventure when the year of loving dangerously begins in July 2000:

July: MISSION: IRRESISTIBLE by Sharon Sala
August: UNDERCOVER BRIDE by Kylie Brant
September: NIGHT OF NO RETURN by Eileen Wilks
October: HER SECRET WEAPON by Beverly Barton
November: HERO AT LARGE by Robyn Amos
December: STRANGERS WHEN WE MARRIED by Carla Cassidy
January: THE SPY WHO LOVED HIM by Merline Lovelace
February: SOMEONE TO WATCH OVER HER by Margaret Watson
March: THE ENEMY'S DAUGHTER by Linda Turner
April: THE WAY WE WED by Pat Warren
May: CINDERELLA'S SECRET AGENT by Ingrid Weaver
June: FAMILIAR STRANGER by Sharon Sala

Available only from Silhouette Intimate Moments at your favorite retail outlet.

Where love comes alive™

If you enjoyed what you just read,
then we've got an offer you can't resist!

Take 2 bestselling
love stories FREE!
Plus get a FREE surprise gift!

Clip this page and mail it to Silhouette Reader Service™

IN U.S.A.	IN CANADA
3010 Walden Ave.	P.O. Box 609
P.O. Box 1867	Fort Erie, Ontario
Buffalo, N.Y. 14240-1867	L2A 5X3

YES! Please send me 2 free Silhouette Intimate Moments® novels and my free surprise gift. Then send me 6 brand-new novels every month, which I will receive months before they're available in stores. In the U.S.A., bill me at the bargain price of $3.80 plus 25¢ delivery per book and applicable sales tax, if any*. In Canada, bill me at the bargain price of $4.21 plus 25¢ delivery per book and applicable taxes**. That's the complete price and a savings of at least 10% off the cover prices—what a great deal! I understand that accepting the 2 free books and gift places me under no obligation ever to buy any books. I can always return a shipment and cancel at any time. Even if I never buy another book from Silhouette, the 2 free books and gift are mine to keep forever. So why not take us up on our invitation. You'll be glad you did!

245 SEN C226
345 SEN C227

Name	(PLEASE PRINT)	
Address	Apt.#	
City	State/Prov.	Zip/Postal Code

* Terms and prices subject to change without notice. Sales tax applicable in N.Y.
** Canadian residents will be charged applicable provincial taxes and GST.
All orders subject to approval. Offer limited to one per household.
® are registered trademarks of Harlequin Enterprises Limited.

INMOM00   ©1998 Harlequin Enterprises Limited

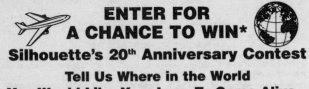

ENTER FOR A CHANCE TO WIN*

Silhouette's 20th Anniversary Contest

Tell Us Where in the World You Would Like *Your* Love To Come Alive... And We'll Send the Lucky Winner There!

Silhouette wants to take you wherever your happy ending can come true.

Here's how to enter: Tell us, in 100 words or less, where you want to go to make your love come alive!

In addition to the grand prize, there will be 200 runner-up prizes, collector's-edition book sets autographed by one of the Silhouette anniversary authors: **Nora Roberts, Diana Palmer, Linda Howard** or **Annette Broadrick**.

DON'T MISS YOUR CHANCE TO WIN! ENTER NOW! No Purchase Necessary

Silhouette®
Where love comes alive™

Visit Silhouette at www.eHarlequin.com to enter, starting this summer.

Name:

Address:

City: State/Province:

Zip/Postal Code:

Mail to Harlequin Books: **In the U.S.**: P.O. Box 9069, Buffalo, NY 14269-9069; **In Canada**: P.O. Box 637, Fort Erie, Ontario, L4A 5X3

SILHOUETTE'S 20ᵀᴴ ANNIVERSARY CONTEST
OFFICIAL RULES
NO PURCHASE NECESSARY TO ENTER

1. To enter, follow directions published in the offer to which you are responding. Contest begins 1/1/00 and ends on 8/24/00 (the "Promotion Period"). Method of entry may vary. Mailed entries must be postmarked by 8/24/00, and received by 8/31/00.

2. During the Promotion Period, the Contest may be presented via the Internet. Entry via the Internet may be restricted to residents of certain geographic areas that are disclosed on the Web site. To enter via the Internet, if you are a resident of a geographic area in which Internet entry is permissible, follow the directions displayed on-line, including typing your essay of 100 words or fewer telling us "Where In The World Your Love Will Come Alive." On-line entries must be received by 11:59 p.m. Eastern Standard time on 8/24/00. Limit one e-mail entry per person, household and e-mail address per day, per presentation. If you are a resident of a geographic area in which entry via the Internet is permissible, you may, in lieu of submitting an entry on-line, enter by mail, by hand-printing your name, address, telephone number and contest number/name on an 8"x 11" plain piece of paper and telling us in 100 words or fewer "Where In The World Your Love Will Come Alive," and mailing via first-class mail to: Silhouette 20ᵗʰ Anniversary Contest, (in the U.S.) P.O. Box 9069, Buffalo, NY 14269-9069; (In Canada) P.O. Box 637, Fort Erie, Ontario, Canada L2A 5X3. Limit one 8"x 11" mailed entry per person, household and e-mail address per day. On-line and/or 8"x 11" mailed entries received from persons residing in geographic areas in which Internet entry is not permissible will be disqualified. No liability is assumed for lost, late, incomplete, inaccurate, nondelivered or misdirected mail, or misdirected e-mail, for technical, hardware or software failures of any kind, lost or unavailable network connection, or failed, incomplete, garbled or delayed computer transmission or any human error which may occur in the receipt or processing of the entries in the contest.

3. Essays will be judged by a panel of members of the Silhouette editorial and marketing staff based on the following criteria:

   > Sincerity (believability, credibility)—50%
   >
   > Originality (freshness, creativity)—30%
   >
   > Aptness (appropriateness to contest ideas)—20%

   Purchase or acceptance of a product offer does not improve your chances of winning. In the event of a tie, duplicate prizes will be awarded.

4. All entries become the property of Harlequin Enterprises Ltd., and will not be returned. Winner will be determined no later than 10/31/00 and will be notified by mail. Grand Prize winner will be required to sign and return Affidavit of Eligibility within 15 days of receipt of notification. Noncompliance within the time period may result in disqualification and an alternative winner may be selected. All municipal, provincial, federal, state and local laws and regulations apply. Contest open only to residents of the U.S. and Canada who are 18 years of age or older, and is void wherever prohibited by law. Internet entry is restricted solely to residents of those geographical areas in which Internet entry is permissible. Employees of Torstar Corp., their affiliates, agents and members of their immediate families are not eligible. Taxes on the prizes are the sole responsibility of winners. Entry and acceptance of any prize offered constitutes permission to use winner's name, photograph or other likeness for the purposes of advertising, trade and promotion on behalf of Torstar Corp. without further compensation to the winner, unless prohibited by law. Torstar Corp and D.L. Blair, Inc., their parents, affiliates and subsidiaries, are not responsible for errors in printing or electronic presentation of contest or entries. In the event of printing or other errors which may result in unintended prize values or duplication of prizes, all affected contest materials or entries shall be null and void. If for any reason the Internet portion of the contest is not capable of running as planned, including infection by computer virus, bugs, tampering, unauthorized intervention, fraud, technical failures, or any other causes beyond the control of Torstar Corp. which corrupt or affect the administration, secrecy, fairness, integrity or proper conduct of the contest, Torstar Corp. reserves the right, at its sole discretion, to disqualify any individual who tampers with the entry process and to cancel, terminate, modify or suspend the contest or the Internet portion thereof. In the event of a dispute regarding an on-line entry, the entry will be deemed submitted by the authorized holder of the e-mail account submitted at the time of entry. Authorized account holder is defined as the natural person who is assigned to an e-mail address by an Internet access provider, on-line service provider or other organization that is responsible for arranging e-mail address for the domain associated with the submitted e-mail address.

5. Prizes: Grand Prize—a $10,000 vacation to anywhere in the world. Travelers (at least one must be 18 years of age or older) or parent or guardian if one traveler is a minor, must sign and return a Release of Liability prior to departure. Travel must be completed by December 31, 2001, and is subject to space and accommodations availability. Two hundred (200) Second Prizes—a two-book limited edition autographed collector set from one of the Silhouette Anniversary authors: Nora Roberts, Diana Palmer, Linda Howard or Annette Broadrick (value $10.00 each set). All prizes are valued in U.S. dollars.

6. For a list of winners (available after 10/31/00), send a self-addressed, stamped envelope to: Harlequin Silhouette 20ᵗʰ Anniversary Winners, P.O. Box 4200, Blair, NE 68009-4200.

Contest sponsored by Torstar Corp., P.O. Box 9042, Buffalo, NY 14269-9042.

PS20RULES